THE

SATURDAY

BOY

THE
SATURDAY
BOY

DAVID
FLEMING

SCHOLASTIC INC.

ISBN 978-0-545-63103-7

Copyright © 2013 by David Fleming.
All rights reserved. Published by Scholastic Inc., 557 Broadway, New York, NY 10012,
by arrangement with Viking, a division of Penguin Young Readers Group,
a member of Penguin Group (USA) Inc. SCHOLASTIC and associated logos
are trademarks and/or registered trademarks of Scholastic Inc.

12 11 10 9 8 7 6 5 4 3   13 14 15 16 17 18/0

Printed in the U.S.A.   23

First Scholastic printing, September 2013

Designed by Jim Hoover
Set in Granjon LT Std

For a mouse,

a monkey,

and a bear.

THE

SATURDAY

BOY

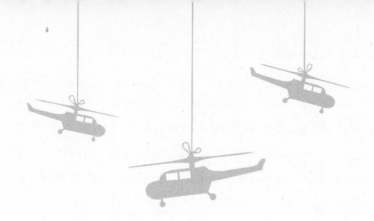

IT WAS A RAINY and cold morning and the bus was late and so was Budgie.

I tried not to think about how cold and wet I was so I thought about superheroes instead. One of them had a cape and could fly. The other had mutant superstrength. There was a burning city and people fleeing in the background and everything.

"Your reign of terror ends here, Richter!"

"That's what you think, Captain Glory! See how you like my earthquake strike!"

Richter clenches his hands over his head and brings them down, striking the ground with enough force to fling Captain Glory into the side of a building like a rag doll. The building shudders and bits of brick and mortar shake loose and fall to the ground. A fire hydrant breaks free from the asphalt, rocketing skyward on a great jet of water, and is lost in a haze of dust and smoke. In seconds, everything is drenched. The fire hydrant lands a block away with a loud *CLANG*!

Richter advances on the fallen Captain Glory, trapping him in the shadow cast by a city in flames. Captain Glory struggles beneath the rubble but can't free himself. Water from the broken pipe rains down as Richter raises his fists a second time and . . . and . . .

Sneezed.

Then he noisily wiped his nose on his sleeve while Captain Glory just lay there shivering in a puddle.

After that all I could think about were wet superheroes. And then cold ones. So I stopped thinking about super-heroes altogether.

Budgie usually wasn't late because Budgie's dad dropped him off every morning on his way to work. Budgie's dad drove a big, silver spy car with leather seats that heated up when you pressed a button and on days like this he'd let me and Budgie sit in the back until the bus came if we promised not to touch anything. It was hard though because there were a *ton* of buttons in the back of Budgie's dad's spy car. One time Budgie said it had an ejector seat but when I asked him where it was he wouldn't tell me. Not even after I offered him the crumble cake from my lunch box. Not even after I *gave* him the crumble cake from my lunch box. Now I don't believe there was ever an ejector seat. I bet there wasn't a button for a smoke screen, either. Or an oil slick. Sometimes I don't like Budgie that much. Sometimes I'd just like to punch him one.

I looked off down the street through the rain. No bus. Then I looked off down the street in the other direction. No Budgie's dad. Man, I could really go for some heated spy car seats, even if it wasn't a *real* spy car. I could go for heated spy car seats even if I had to sit with Budgie, who always smelled like eggs and sometimes punched me in the leg for no reason. I could go for heated spy car seats because I was cold and starting to shiver.

A car pulled up next to me but it wasn't a spy car. It was a minivan—a boring old minivan with boring, old, non-heated, regular backseats. It beeped at me so I moved over and stepped right into a puddle and now my sneakers were filling up with water. Now I'd have to dry my socks and shoes on the radiator and sit at my desk with cold pruney-raisin feet and probably miss recess. The window rolled down and I heard someone say my name.

"Derek?"

It was Budgie's mom. Budgie was in the backseat laughing and holding his belly as if his guts were about to pop out all over the car. His face was red and wobbly. He looked like a big tomato.

Budgie's mom got out of the car with an umbrella and

came around and opened the door and I got in. I was dripping water everyplace like I was melting and my book bag was soaked and probably my books were, too.

Budgie laughed so hard he farted.

"Derek?" Budgie's mom asked.

"Yes?"

"What are you doing in the rain?"

"Waiting for the bus," I said.

"Derek?" Budgie's mom asked.

"Yes?"

"It's Saturday."

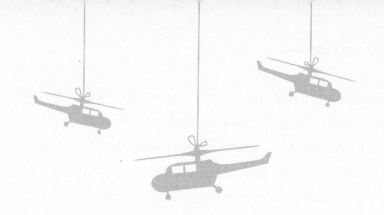

INSTEAD OF TAKING ME home right away, Budgie's mom drove to the ice rink to drop Budgie off for hockey practice because they were already running late. On the way, Budgie's mom called my mom on her cell phone and told her about me and the bus stop and said she didn't see how I could have gotten ready for school *and* left the house *and* been standing at the bus stop in the *rain* for *so* long without anybody noticing and that she wasn't judging, she was just saying.

"I know it must be difficult, Annie," she said, "given your, well, you know—your *circumstances.*"

But Budgie's mom didn't know. She was just one of those people who said they did. I got the feeling that sometimes the people who said they knew everything actually knew way less than everybody else. If that was true, then Budgie's mom was some kind of reverse genius.

Budgie laughed at me all the way to the ice rink. Weird squeaking noises came out of him as he held his belly and

I kinda wished his guts *would* pop out all over the car. He was going to tell everyone at school, I just knew it. By recess time on Monday, they'd be calling me "ducky-boy" or "puddle-duck" and they'd quack at me when I passed them in the hall or something. Monday was going to be bad. Maybe I could get a cold before then.

At my house, my mom waved to Budgie's mom from the doorway but Budgie's mom drove away without waving back. Because she had to drive me home she was going to be late for her hair appointment and if she was late for her hair appointment they might cancel it altogether and if that happened then her whole day would be ruined and it would be the end of the world. I might have left something out but that's mostly what she told me.

Mom leaned against the washing machine in the mudroom and tucked her hair back. Normally her frizzy curls were tied back in a ponytail or a braid because of work, but this morning they were wild and free. When she asked what she was going to do with me, I suggested she give me a dollar. She smiled at that, which made me happy. Mom didn't smile much anymore. Well, she did but most of the time it was like something was missing. You could tell.

"What happened this morning?"

"I don't want to tell you."

"Why?"

"Because it's stupid," I said. "I—it's embarrassing."

"Don't be embarrassed. It's me."

"You won't laugh?"

"Why would I—of course not!"

"I thought it was Friday."

"When?"

"When I woke up this morning. I—hey! You said you wouldn't laugh!"

"I'm not!"

"You are! You're *totally* laughing at me!"

"I am not. I'm . . . snickering."

"Well stop."

"Sorry."

"Because it's not like it never happened to you."

"You're right. I'm sorry. Please continue."

"When I woke up you were still sleeping and I didn't want to bother you because I know you've been working a lot lately. So I got myself ready. And I went. By myself. So you could sleep. It was really very thoughtful of me."

"Yes, it was, Piggy, *very* thoughtful. And I'm sorry." She poked my belly and tweaked my nose—a thing she used to do when I was little. "I'm sorry it rained on you, and I'm sorry you caught Budgie's mom in a bad mood when you were just trying to do something nice for me."

"Apology accepted," I said, tweaking her nose in return.

"And you shouldn't worry about me like that when I'm sure you have big, important eleven-year-old things to think about instead, right?"

I shrugged. She *was* right. I did have important eleven-year-old things to think about. Lots of them. But they weren't going to stop me from worrying about her sometimes. I didn't tell her that, though, because as much as she didn't want me to worry about her—I didn't want her to worry about me.

"Oh yeah," I said. "Buttloads."

"Really? Buttloads? You're going with that?"

I told her I was.

She hugged me tight, told me she loved me and to run upstairs and towel off and put on some dry clothes so I wouldn't catch a cold. I found an extra-fluffy towel in the linen closet in the upstairs hallway. It was in the middle of the stack and when I pulled it out the whole thing toppled over. I tried to put them back the way Mom had but it didn't look the same. Finally I just shoved them up on the shelf in a pile, closed the door, and went to my room to dry off.

The first thing I did when I came through the door was go up on my toes and touch the model P-51 Mustang fighter plane that hung from the ceiling so it would swing back and forth. I did the same to the Hawker Hurricane so it looked like the two planes were fighting. Man, if I had a big fan I'd turn it on so it would look like *all* my fighter aircraft models were flying around in a huge air battle. Every time I pictured it, though, the Apache helicopter always won.

The Apache is my favorite because it's like the one my dad pilots. He surprised me with the model the last time he was home and we built it together. Sometimes when I can't sleep, I stare up at it and pretend it's a real helicopter, and me and Dad are in it flying top secret missions and battling the forces of evil to save the world. And we have cool code names and sunglasses. Before he left we hung the Apache helicopter model right over my head so it would be the first thing I saw when I woke up. That was a long time ago.

On Monday Mom drove me to school because I missed the bus and by the time I got there everybody knew about what happened on Saturday. I put my lunch box and my jacket in my cubby in the hallway and looked through the little window in the door. I could see Budgie and the rest of the class doing the morning assignment. Budgie must have noticed me in the window because he looked up from his work and smiled.

"Hey, Saturday boy!" he said as I opened the door.

I didn't say anything. Instead I went to my seat and sat

down and looked at the whiteboard. There was a sentence written on it that read, "Gracie, my dog, ate her dinner."

There were other words, too. Words like "subject" and "verb" and "appositive"—names of things I was supposed to identify when diagramming the sentence. I opened my desk to get a pencil so I could get started but I couldn't find one. I looked around the room but everybody was busy and it was very quiet. They'd all be done soon and Ms. Dickson would come around to check our work, only I wouldn't have any work to check and then what?

She'd make an example of me is what.

Ms. Dickson loved making examples of me. One time she made me come to the front of the class and sit in an empty seat right next to her desk for the whole day. Then there was the time she caught me with a note and I had to write "I will not write notes in class" over and over on the whiteboard while she went on teaching. I bet this time she'd put me in the stocks and have the class throw tomatoes at me. She had a good imagination when it came to stuff like that.

I looked around and saw Ms. Dickson two rows away and steadily closing in. Luckily she was old and didn't move very fast. One time Budgie told me that if you listened carefully you could hear her creak when she walked, but I didn't believe him. At least I'd never heard any creaking and I'm a pretty good listener.

I searched through my desk. Where was my pencil? I was starting to think maybe Budgie had taken it so I'd get in trouble. I tell you, if I had some knockout drops and rope and a whole bunch of itching powder I'd fix his wagon real good. Or I could just tape a big bug inside his underwear.

Then I saw something move out of the corner of my eye. It was the new girl and she was waving her hand at me. I think maybe she'd said something, too.

"Hm?"

"I said do you need to borrow a pencil?"

Her name was Violet and she sat in the row next to me. She wasn't like the other girls in my class. I couldn't tell you how, exactly, she just wasn't. The other girls were screechy and chirpy and traveled in flocks. But not Violet.

"Pencil?"

"Oh, just take it!"

Pencil? Yes! Pencil! And it didn't even matter that it was girly with cupids on it or that the eraser was all pink and heart-shaped. I didn't even care if everyone saw me writing with a girl's pencil. I'm using a girl's pencil! I got out a piece of paper and wrote so fast and hard that the point broke off.

"Derek!"

I jumped. Ms. Dickson had snuck up on me.

"Well *this* is interesting," she said. "I think perhaps we should share this with the rest of the class."

Ms. Dickson took my paper to the front of the class. I looked around the room. Everybody was looking at me and for once it wasn't because I'd spoken out of turn or started babbling on about superheroes. This was different. This was the good kind of being looked at.

Then I looked at the whiteboard and so did the other kids and then they were looking at me again but this time they were looking at me the way they usually do. Then they started laughing. Ms. Dickson had erased the sentence about Gracie and her dinner and written a new one in its place. It read, "I'm using a girl's pencil."

And then, to my horror, she had me come up to the front of the room and diagram it.

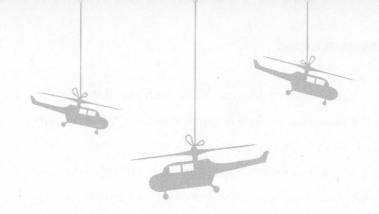

THAT DAY AFTER SCHOOL I went to my hideout. But not right away. I went home first and had a snack but I was still angry so I didn't really like it as much as I could have even if it *was* a Chocolate Ka-Blam and Chocolate Ka-Blams were usually my favorite.

My hideout was in the loft in the garage. I'd stacked up a bunch of boxes so you couldn't see me from below, and if I pulled the ladder up, then there was no getting to me at all. I was totally safe. Except for the time I saw a fiddleback spider. That time I didn't really feel safe at all. That time freaked me out and I didn't go back for a month.

I had a milk crate to sit on and an old coat that I could put on in case I got cold. There was a skylight pretty much right over my head so I could read the comics that I kept in a plastic box. They were all alphabetized and individually wrapped. Sometimes instead of taking them out of the box I'd just run my fingertips along the top of them and listen to them rustle together.

They were treasures. Mine and my dad's and even
some of *his* dad's—*Red Vengeance* number one, for example.
Also *Gumshoe Comics* number fourteen featuring the first
appearance of Guttersnipe, and issue twenty-three of *The
Marvelous Magpie* where her secret identity is revealed.
These weren't just classic issues. They were frickin' *epic*.

I opened the box and got out a comic and tried to read but
couldn't even though it was my favorite issue of *The Exilers*.
Instead I sat on the milk crate and felt mad about things. I
felt mad that Ms. Dickson had put my sentence about Violet's
girly pencil on the board where everyone could see it and I
felt mad that everyone saw it. I felt especially mad at Budgie
because whenever he got the chance after that he'd put on
this high, girly voice and ask to borrow my pencil. Then
when we were playing dodgeball during gym class he asked
me if I had hearts on my panties and when I told him I didn't
wear panties he pulled my pants down.

Mom said I should turn the other cheek and be the
bigger person and that Budgie only acts that way because
there's sadness in his life that makes him scared and insecure. I didn't know if that was true and even if it was that
still didn't make it okay. So I sat there for a long time not
reading comics and just being mad. Then I remembered I
had some paper and a pen in the box and I got them out
and started writing.

Dear Dad,

    How are you?

    Today was really good.

    Ms. Dickson put my sentance on the board because she thought it was the best one. In gym class we played dogeball and I didn't get out once. I even caught the ball when Budgie tried to get me out and everybody cheered. They carried me around on their sholders and everything. It was cool. Coach even said I could be a pro so you don't have to worry about me. I'm doing fine. I can take care of mom with dogeball money.

Love,

Derek

I was in my hideout for so long that when Mom finally called me in for dinner the sky had started to change colors. It wasn't really daytime anymore. But it wasn't really night-time, either. It was that weird, quiet place in between.

Me and Mom had spaghetti for dinner and by the time I was done eating and had gotten ready for bed and watched the new episode of *Zeroman* I'd pretty much forgotten all about Budgie and Violet's girly pencil and the underwear incident. But once I got in bed and turned out the light I wound up staring at the Apache helicopter for what seemed like forever.

Me and Dad are buzzing over the desert with two Spitfires hot on our tail. Their machine guns are blazing. *RAT-A-TATTA-TAT! RAT-A-TATTA-TAT!* I weave in and out and in between the bullets as they streak past, barely missing us. My code name is Stingray. I'm wearing pilot sunglasses and chewing on a toothpick. Dad is in front of me in the gunner's seat, his head moving back and forth as he looks for targets.

"These bogies're getting close, Stingray!" Dad shouts, his voice crackling in my headset. "We can't outrun them much longer!"

"Time to go upstairs!" I shout back.

"What? You're crazy!"

"Hang on!"

I pull back on the stick as far as she'll go and the chopper starts to climb into the air as the g-force pushes us down into our seats. The stick's wobbling like mad. I grit my teeth and hold on, biting the toothpick in half. The chopper climbs, climbs, goes upside down and starts to descend. Bright lights flash in my field of vision and as I start to slip into the black I hear a voice—Dad's voice.

"Dammit, Stingray, hang on! I can't do this by myself!"

Amazingly, I snap out of it. The Spitfires are ahead of

us now. I can picture the pilots looking around, wondering where we went. Dad's finger slips around the trigger of the Apache's thirty-millimeter chain gun. *RAT-A-TATTA-TATTA-TAT-BOOM! RAT-A-TATTA-TATTA-TAT-BOOM!* The chopper slices through the cloud of smoke, leaving the Spitfires' pilots behind, parachuting down and shaking their fists at us.

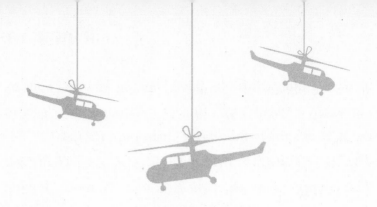

"HEY, SATURDAY BOY," Budgie said the next morning at the bus stop. "What's on your panties today? Unicorns?"

I wanted to tell him shut up and that I wasn't wearing unicorn underwear. I wanted to tell him that I didn't even *have* unicorn underwear. I wanted to tell him that my underwear was better than his because mine had robots and his probably just had skid marks, but I didn't. I was going to be the bigger person instead. And being the bigger person I decided to help because I figured that's what bigger people did.

"You're only acting like that because there's pain in your life," I told him.

"What? No there's not!"

"Yes there is. And you're scared and insecure and that's why you're such a fudgebag."

Budgie's face went blank and I continued to be the bigger person by ignoring him. The bus came and we got on and he still hadn't said anything. He just looked confused. On the way to school this little kid called Ellory barfed up his pancakes all over the place so Budgie spent most of the time making fun of him and by the time we got to school he'd completely forgotten about me.

Ms. Dickson was sitting at her desk when we got to the classroom and after everybody had taken their seats she did roll call. I remembered this one time Ms. Dickson said it was time to call the roll and Budgie said, "Here, roll! Come here, boy! Good roll!"

Even Ms. Dickson had laughed and that never happened. I tried it the next day and got in trouble. Nobody laughed, either. Maybe I said it wrong.

When Ms. Dickson had finished she picked Missy Sprout to take the attendance sheet to the office. She always picked Missy Sprout to do stuff like that but I couldn't figure out why. It's not like she was fast or anything. I bet I could take the attendance sheet to the office and be back a lot faster than Missy Sprout ever could. I wouldn't stop for anything or anyone—not even the hall monitor. Missy Sprout takes so long I bet she stops for tea and crumpets with everyone she sees.

"Now," said Ms. Dickson, "do any of you know who Charles Dickens is?"

"Your husband!"

"No, Budgie."

"Your brother!"

Ms. Dickson pinched the top of her nose and closed her eyes. Then she took a deep breath and let it out.

"Let's try this another way," she said. "Do any of you know *A Christmas Carol*?"

"'Jingle Bells'!"

"Somebody other than Budgie, maybe?" said Ms. Dickson. "Somebody with their hand up? Violet?"

"Charles Dickens was an author," Violet said.

"That is correct," said Ms. Dickson.

Then she asked Violet if she knew what *A Christmas Carol* was about and Violet said she did, so Ms. Dickson asked her to share with the class and she did.

I liked the sound of Violet's voice and the way she said things. I listened to her tell about this mean, old miserly guy called Scrooge and how he had this guy who worked for him named Cratchit and how Scrooge wanted him to work all night but the guy didn't want to because he had a son named Tiny Tim who was really sick and it was Christmas Eve outside. Then she told about how when Scrooge got home he was visited by the ghost of Bob Marley who said there were going to be three more ghosts and they were all going to show him different stuff and they did and in the morning it was Christmas and Scrooge bought a turkey.

"That was very good, Violet," said Ms. Dickson. "Now, at the end of next month Mr. Putnam and the middle school drama club will be putting on a play of *A Christmas Carol* and he told me he needs two volunteers, one boy and one girl, to be in it."

I knew what a play was. My mom and dad took me to one once. I don't really remember the name of it but everyone was dressed up like cats. The Christmas carol play sounded good, though. It had ghosts. Maybe I could be one of them. Being a ghost would be cool. Violet's hand was already up. She'd raised it even before Ms. Dickson had finished talking. I put my hand up, too. Mostly so Violet's wouldn't be lonely.

I could feel everybody looking at me. They were probably looking at Violet, too. I looked down at my desk and felt my face get all warm. Out of the corner of my eye I could see Violet. She was smiling like she wasn't bothered by the stares and giggles. Maybe she wasn't. Then Violet was smiling at me and I was smiling back. It felt pretty good.

Later that day when we came in from recess there was a note on my desk from Budgie that said,

Derek loves Vilet.

He didn't sign it or anything but Budgie isn't very good at spelling so I knew it was probably him. I looked around to tell him he was wrong but he was talking with this kid named Barely O'Donahue. His real name was Barry but pretty much everybody called him Barely because he was so short. I crushed up Budgie's note and put it in my desk.

During the last period Sally, who sits behind me, passed me a note. It was from Budgie. Nobody good ever passed me notes. It said,

You

I looked over my shoulder at Budgie but he had his head down and he was working. Was that it? Where was the rest of it? That was the worst note ever. I put it in my desk and went back to drawing superheroes in the margins of my math book. About a minute later Sally passed me another note. This one said,

You love

My face started to feel hot all of a sudden. I shoved the note into my desk before anyone could see. I drew Budgie as a big, fat, marshmallow thing with legs and I drew Bonfyre roasting it with her fire bolts. I also added a couple of Boy Scouts who were waiting around to make s'mores out of him. They had a box of graham crackers and everything. Then Sally passed me another note. I should have just put it in my desk without looking at it. I should have eaten it or burned it or done anything but open it but I opened it. In Budgie's big, stupid handwriting it read,

You love her!!!!!!

I crumpled up the note, spun around in my seat, and whipped it at Budgie.

"*Eat it,* fat boy!"

Everything stopped. Ms. Dickson stopped writing on the whiteboard. Everyone stopped working. I think even the clock stopped ticking. Budgie held his hand over his eye like he was hurt even though I could tell he was totally faking. I knew it was wrong but I kinda wished he was hurt for real. Turning the other cheek all the time was hard work. What did they think? That I was made of them?

"Derek! Office! Now!"

Of course. Because it was *my* fault.

I stopped in the boys' room on the way to the office to splash some cold water on my face because all the unfairness had gotten me all hot and mad. I plugged the drain with a paper towel and turned on the cold water in the sink. When it was full I turned the water off. I splashed some on my face and that helped a little but I was still thinking about Budgie sitting there holding his eye like he was hurt and I bet I didn't even hit him. I bet everyone was paying attention to him and feeling bad for him and suddenly I was mad again so I took a deep breath and dunked my head in the sink as far as it would go.

When I pulled my head out of the sink cold water splashed down my neck and onto the front of my shirt and even though I didn't really feel angry anymore, I was still in trouble and now I was wet. I got a paper towel and dried my face and threw it out. Then I got another one and dried my neck and threw that one out. Then I got *another* one and started drying my hair. Ms. Dickson would have said I was dawdling.

The way I saw it, I was just taking the time to do a good job.

I was doing such a good job, in fact, that when the end-of-the-day bell rang I was still standing there. I swallowed hard, suddenly feeling like I'd been gutpunched.

I'd completely forgotten to go to the principal's office.

I was toast. I was dead. I was worse than dead—I was

doomed. Making a mess in the boys' room and using all the paper towels was one thing, but disobeying a teacher when they'd told you to do something was another. Forget sitting next to the teacher's desk or writing something over and over again on the whiteboard until you couldn't feel your hand anymore, this time Ms. Dickson was going to kill me.

What was I going to do? I couldn't get killed now. What would I say to my mom?

I opened the bathroom door and peeked into the hallway. The doors to the classrooms were open and kids were coming out to get their coats and get ready to go outside to catch the buses. Man, it would be good to be one of those kids right about now. I'd be putting my jacket on and be thinking about Chocolate Ka-Blams and *Zeroman* instead of hiding out in the boys' room with damp hair and no more paper towels.

I had to think of something quick. Kids were starting to stream down the hall past the bathroom and it wasn't like I could just step out and join them. I didn't have my backpack or my jacket, and besides, if Budgie saw me he'd dime me out for sure. I'd have to wait. I couldn't go home without my stuff and I couldn't get my stuff until Ms. Dickson and the class had gone.

I really wanted to stick my head out to see where Ms.

Dickson and the rest of the class were but I knew that would be a bad idea so I didn't. Luckily I heard Budgie's fat, dumb laugh coming from down the hall. Somebody must have told him the one about the chicken crossing the road because he's the only one in the whole world who thinks it's funny. I closed the door and waited until I couldn't hear his laugh anymore and when I opened the door again the hallway was empty.

This was it.

I snuck down the hall and into the classroom. Through the windows I could see the turnaround where the buses were lining up with all the kids waiting to get on. I didn't have much time. Soon the buses would be full and they'd drive away and I'd be stuck here. I grabbed all my stuff and was pulling on my jacket when I noticed that Budgie had left his math workbook on his desk.

Budgie. Budgie with the fat, dumb laugh. Budgie whose fault this all was.

I went over and picked up the book and flipped through it a little. We had math homework tonight and he couldn't do it without the book. The nice thing to do would be to bring it to him. The right thing to do would be to bring it to him. He could get in trouble if he didn't do his homework.

I looked out the window again. The buses were filling

up. I thought about Budgie and what Mom had said about him having pain in his life. Then I thought about what a pain it was having him in *my* life. I thought about those two things for as long as I could without missing the bus.

Then I glued the book to his desk and ran.

Mom was waiting for me when I got home.

"Derek?"

"Yeah?"

I dropped my backpack on the floor and took off my jacket and hung it up and went into the pantry for a Chocolate Ka-Blam. When I turned around Mom was standing in the doorway. Her arms were crossed. She didn't look happy. She looked disappointed and a little sad.

"Do you know who I just got off the phone with?"

"No."

"Derek."

"Ms. Dickson?"

"*And* Mr. Howard," said Mom. "Do you know why they called?"

I nodded and fiddled with the Chocolate Ka-Blam and then put it back on the shelf. I suddenly wasn't very hungry anymore.

I remembered the last thing Mr. Howard had called

about. It was easy to remember because Dad had just gotten home and I always remembered everything that happened when he was here.

It'd been late and I was supposed to be in bed but I'd had two sodas at the welcome home party and they'd had caffeine in them so I sat at the bottom of the stairs instead, listening to my daddy's voice as he and Mom talked in the kitchen.

I didn't know what they were talking about and it didn't matter. I'd just missed the sound of my dad's voice. My mom once said she thought Dad must be afraid of the quiet the way he was always talking to himself and singing but I didn't agree. My dad's not afraid of anything. But the quiet is awfully loud when he's away.

I didn't remember how long I'd been sitting there listening but at some point the tone of my dad's voice changed and I started to pay attention. He was angry. I hoped it wasn't because of me.

"What? No. No way. We've been through this once already."

"We have, Jason, but—"

"Remember first grade? His teacher *decided* there was something wrong with him and wouldn't shut up about it until we agreed to have him tested?"

I didn't remember taking any tests or anything but first grade was ages ago.

"And even after everything came back negative she *still* wouldn't let it go?"

"I remember. I do. Just—"

"Annie, c'mon," Dad said. "That's messed up."

"Yes it is."

"Why can't he just be a high-spirited kid? Why do people feel the need to put labels on everything?" Dad said. "You want a label for Derek? Awesome. There it is. There's your label."

I totally remember him saying that. Word for word. Mom agreed, saying something like if Dad was trying to get an argument out of her he'd have to try harder. Then she said, "Mr. Howard said Derek's in a different kind of trouble. There have been a few . . . outbursts."

First of all, those had *not* been my fault. If Mrs. Bailey hadn't spent so much time with her back to the classroom she'd have *seen* all the stuff that went down—all the spitballs and ear flicks—but that wasn't the case. All she'd heard were the times I'd reacted. Because she was always facing the whiteboard she'd missed all the times I *did* ignore them—all the times I *hadn't* done anything.

She'd missed all the times I'd just sat there and taken it.

"What have they decided is the matter this time?"

"Don't be like that, Jason," Mom said. "It's not like the teachers *want* him to fail."

"How should I be then?" said Dad. He was frowning. I could hear it in his voice. "This is *exactly* what I was afraid of. It got written down in some file that *one* teacher *thought* there was a problem and now that red flag's always going to be there. I'm sorry. It just frustrates the hell out of me that he has to deal with this. Again. It sucks."

I remember him saying that because it was a word that I wasn't allowed to use. But it *did* suck. It sucked a lot. I sat on the stairs then, feeling angry and frustrated at the unfairness—the *suckiness*—of it all. Feeling like there was nothing I could do.

"You're right. It completely sucks. But it happened."

"Did your sister ever have to deal with anything like this?"

"Like what?"

"People thinking she had a problem or was strange because of the way she dressed or the music she was into or whatever," Dad said. "Don't forget—I've seen Josie's Mohawk pictures from high school."

I remember wondering how anybody could think Aunt Josie was strange. There was just no way. Maybe they were just jealous of how cool she was. Not everybody got to be an artist, after all, and I bet the number of people who got to be tattoo artists was even smaller. She'd also lived in Mexico and Japan and just about every time she came over she'd give me a new tattoo with Magic Markers. I was her favorite client because I sat like a rock. That's what she told me.

". . . and right or wrong people are going to have their opinions of him," Mom was saying. "They're going to label him in the same way they felt the need to label my sister and everything else—because their world doesn't make sense without them.

"Listen—Derek has proven them wrong before. Just have him meet with their behaviorist and he'll do it again and we can move on. Okay?" I remember hearing her chair scrape on the kitchen floor and her footsteps as she walked around the table. I knew she'd sat in my dad's lap because his chair made a noise like it was complaining. "Would you like to know what I think?"

"Yes I would," my dad said.

"I think he missed his daddy. Plain and simple. He puts on a brave face but I can tell it's tough for him when you're not here. He needed you."

"Well, he's got me," Dad said. "I'm home now."

"Why are you smiling?" Mom asked, smashing the memory to pieces and yanking me back to the present. "Is this funny to you? I asked you if you knew why they called."

"Ms. Dickson told me to go to the office and I didn't go," I said.

"Why not?"

"I was going to, I swear," I said. "But I went to the boys' room and I lost track of time."

"What were you doing in the boys' room?"

"Drying my hair."

"Drying your—wait. What?"

So I told her. Then I told her about what happened—about Budgie and the notes he'd passed me and that it was impossible for me to love Violet because I barely even knew her. All I knew for sure was that she used a pencil with a heart-shaped eraser and every Friday she smelled like apples. That was it.

"Ms. Dickson didn't mention Budgie," Mom said.

"See, it's not my fault!"

"Derek, just because it's *not* your fault doesn't mean you're not *at* fault," Mom said. "What you did today was very dangerous. Do you understand why?"

I looked at the floor and thought for a second.

"I guess maybe I could have slipped and hit my head," I said.

"No," Mom said. "Well, yes, that's part of it. You *could* have hit your head, but more importantly, nobody would have known you were hurt and needed help. Does that make sense?"

I nodded.

"I promised Ms. Dickson and Mr. Howard I would talk to you about this but I wouldn't be surprised if there were some repercussions at school tomorrow."

"What, like drums?"

"Drums?"

"Yeah," I said. "Percussion. That's like drums, right?"

Mom smiled.

"Yes, percussion is like drums but I said repercussions, which are like consequences."

I would have preferred drums. Drums were way better than consequences.

"And as far as that—as far as Budgie goes . . . just try to be the bigger person, okay? Try to ignore him?"

I told her I would but that trying to ignore Budgie was like trying to ignore a flaming elephant. Mom smiled again and laughed a little through her nose. I smiled, too, and that's how I knew we were going to be okay.

"I'm sorry about today, Mom," I said. "I'll do better."

"I know you will, Piggy-pig," she said. She roughed up my hair, which was totally dry now.

I picked up the Chocolate Ka-Blam after all and went up to my bedroom and lay on my bed and ate it. Then I got out some paper and a pen.

Dear Dad,

Today Ms. Dickson picked me out of the whole class to be in a play with the middle school drama club. It's called a chrismas carol and it has ghosts in it. I think all plays should have ghosts. Violet is in it to. Maybe we will get to be ghosts. Also I got in trouble today for throwing something at Budgie. Last night on Zeroman doctor Mayhem was going to posion the water supply with Serum Z that would turn everyone into zombies but Zeroman flew in and fot him and destroyed the serum. It was cool. When you come home we can watch it together.

Love

derek

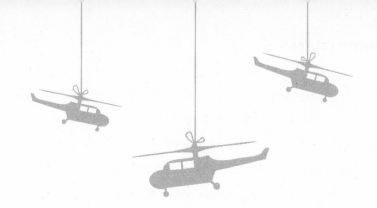

A COUPLE OF DAYS went by and nothing much happened. Then one morning I missed the bus and Mom had to drive me to school and when I got to the classroom everybody was crowded around Budgie.

"What's going on?" I asked Barely O'Donahue.

"Budgie climbed the tree!"

There wasn't a kid in school who didn't know about the tree. It had silver bark and purply, reddish leaves and was a hundred feet tall. Maybe even two hundred. It was off limits because one time a kid fell out and broke his neck and turned into a vegetable but sometimes kids climbed it anyway when no one was looking.

"He even carved his name on the top branch with a knife!"

"No he didn't," I said.

"Yes he did!"

"No way."

"Yes way," Barely O'Donahue said. "Curds and way."

Then Ms. Dickson told us all to sit down and I tried to listen to what she was saying but I kept thinking about Budgie and the tree and how I didn't believe any of it because Budgie had about as much natural climbing ability as a walrus no matter what Barely O'Donahue said.

I looked around at Budgie. He was sitting at his desk looking more puffed up than usual. I bet he hadn't climbed the tree at all. I bet he was giving Barely O'Donahue candy or cookies just to say he did. I was also pretty sure he didn't carve his name on any branch. As far as I knew he didn't even *have* a pocketknife.

Budgie found me on the monkey bars during recess. Barely O'Donahue and a couple other kids were with him.

"Barely says you don't believe I climbed the tree," he said.

I looked down from the monkey bars at him. Barley seemed even smaller from up there.

"So?"

"So *do* you?"

"Do I what?"

"Do you believe I climbed the tree?"

More kids were coming over. They quit playing tag. They stopped playing four square and crackabout and wall ball. I don't know why I said what I said next. Maybe it was because Budgie was surrounded by kids who thought he was some kind of hero when he hadn't done anything except lie to them and that didn't seem right. Maybe I thought I could get away with it because there were so many people around. Or maybe the words just popped into my head and they came out before I could stop them.

"Dude, I don't believe you could climb *any* tree."

Some of the kids laughed including Barely O'Donahue. Budgie didn't laugh. His face went red instead.

"What did you just say?"

"He said he didn't believe you could climb any tree," said Barely O'Donahue.

"I heard him."

"You know, because you're fat."

"Shut up!"

Now just about everyone was laughing. Budgie's face got redder—almost purple.

"Are you saying you could do better?" he asked.

Budgie stood below the monkey bars waiting for me to answer. I looked around at the kids. They were waiting for an answer, too. There was really only one thing I could say so I said it.

"Yeah."

The kids in the crowd all started talking between each

other and Budgie stood there with his arms crossed and a mean grin on his face. My mouth went dry all of a sudden. What if he *hadn't* made the whole thing up?

"After school," he said. "At the tree."

Then he turned around and walked away and Barely O'Donahue and a couple of other kids followed him. The kids who were left walked away, too. They started playing four square and crackabout and wall ball again. I was all alone on top of the monkey bars wondering if I hadn't just made the biggest mistake of my life.

Normally I couldn't wait for the day to be over. Normally I'd be counting down the minutes until the bell. Today was not a normal day. Today I actually wished the clock would slow down. Sally passed me a note and I opened it even though I knew I shouldn't have. At first I thought Budgie's drawing was of a weasel falling off a burning flagpole, then I realized it wasn't a burning flagpole at all. It was a tree. And if the burning flagpole was a tree, that meant I was the weasel.

I wanted to turn around and scream at him that nobody believed he'd climbed the stupid tree anyway and that I didn't have to prove anything to him or anybody else and that nobody liked him or cared about what he said, including Barely O'Donahue, who probably only hung around because he was short and afraid of being picked on. Instead I crumpled up the note and put it in my desk, which is what I should have done in the first place.

The clock kept ticking. The bell would ring soon and the day would end and I'd have to climb the tree and I wasn't very good at climbing trees. But just because I wasn't that good at it didn't mean I was scared to. Budgie would soon find out that Derek Lamb was no chicken. Plus about a thousand people heard me say I'd do it.

"All right, Lamb, up you go."

Me, Budgie, Barely O'Donahue, and a few kids from recess were all standing at the bottom of the tree looking up. I could see part of the sky and some clouds through the branches. They seemed very far away.

"What branch?" I asked.

"What what branch?" said Budgie.

"What branch did you carve your name on?"

Budgie glanced at Barely O'Donahue, who shrugged and shook his head.

"You know—the top one," said Budgie.

"There's more than one branch at the top."

"Quit stalling!"

I wasn't stalling. How could Budgie expect me to climb higher than he did if he couldn't even remember which branch he carved his name on? I know that if it was me I'd totally remember. If it was me I would've hung a flag and claimed the tree for Derekland.

"Go on, Captain Saturday, get up there!" said Budgie.

"Yeah, go on!" said Barely O'Donahue. "Whatcha waiting for?"

"What's the matter, Lamb? Chicken?"

I laughed. I couldn't help it.

"Dude, you sound like that dog food commercial."

"What?"

Now I was stalling. I figured the longer I put it off, the more likely we'd get caught and I wouldn't have to do it at all.

"You know—the Hungry Pup commercial? With that song?"

"*I* know that one!" said Barely O'Donahue.

"If your pup is up and sniffin' in the kitchen," I sang, with Barely O'Donahue and a couple of the other kids joining in. "Hungry Pup's got rice, lamb, and chicken!"

"What are you doing?" asked Budgie angrily.

"What?" answered Barely O'Donahue. "It's a commercial."

"I know it's a commercial."

I looked up at the school building while Budgie and

Barely O'Donahue worked things out, hoping we'd be spotted by a teacher or a janitor—somebody, *anybody* with even the slightest bit of authority who might recognize this as a potential breaking of the rules.

"What're you doing now?" said Budgie.

"Making sure there's no teachers," I said. "You wanna get busted?"

"Just hurry up!"

I looked up into the tree again and swallowed hard. Three hundred feet. At least.

Ignoring Budgie, Barely O'Donahue, and the others, I walked around the tree looking for a good place to start. Luckily, the tree had some branches close to the ground and I found a sturdy one and climbed up onto it. From there I found another branch a little farther up. It was narrower than the first one but still wide enough for both feet and I hugged the trunk and pressed my cheek against the bark. My hands were starting to sweat and I hoped that Budgie couldn't see that my legs were shaking.

"That branch looks wobbly," said Budgie. "Are you sure it'll hold you?"

"It held you, didn't it?"

Some of the kids laughed.

"What did you just say?"

"He said, 'It held you, didn't it,'" said Barely O'Donahue.

"I heard him."

"You know, because you're fat."

"Shut up!"

I tried not to listen to Budgie. I tried not to listen to Barely O'Donahue. I'd discovered something I didn't want to do more than climb the tree and that was fall out of it. My heart was pounding so loud I was pretty sure Budgie could hear it.

"You suck, Lamb!" he said.

"Rack of lamb!" said Barely O'Donahue. "Ram-a-lamb-a-ding-dong!"

I kept going. I'd stopped thinking about it. I was just climbing—grabbing one branch after another, hoisting, pulling myself higher into the tree. I kept an eye out for Budgie's name even though the higher I got, the more I believed it wasn't there.

I got to a place where I could balance pretty good and stopped to catch my breath. My hands hurt. They were dirty and shaky and hard to open. I didn't know how high up I was but I couldn't see Budgie anymore because there were too many leaves in the way. Come to think of it, I hadn't heard him for a while either.

I did hear something though. It sounded like bus engines.

"Budgie," I shouted down, "do you hear the bus?"

Mom was working a late shift today, which meant my aunt Josie would be at my house, and since her car was still getting fixed it meant if I missed the bus I would have no way of getting home. I couldn't miss the bus. I just couldn't.

"Budgie?"

My stomach dropped. Budgie wasn't there anymore, I just knew it.

And if Budgie wasn't there, then Barely O'Donahue and the other kids weren't there either. They were probably in line for the bus already. They might even be *on* the bus. I pictured them sitting in the way back, yucking it up, giving each other high-fives for ditching me.

They were a clever bunch for sure.

I climbed down as fast as I could. My feet slipped on the branches and some of them bent and broke but I hung on. My shirt ripped. Branches poked at me. Leaves swirled around me. My foot got stuck and I unstuck it. I could feel something in my hair—leaves or twigs maybe—and something itching me on my back. I hoped it wasn't spiders. When I thought I was close enough to the ground to not get hurt, I took a deep breath and flung myself outward.

As I fell through the air I heard my dad's voice, recalling the words of his commanding officer from a story he told me about his first day of jump school.

"Landing is easy. All's you need to remember are the following three words in the following order." I pictured my dad's CO wearing mirrored sunglasses and chewing on a cigar, voice raspy from a lifetime of barking orders. "Feet. Ass. Head."

I hit the ground pretty hard but in the correct order, little darts of pain shooting up my legs even though I remembered to bend my knees. I grabbed my bag and my jacket, thankful that Budgie hadn't thought to hide them or, worse, open my bag and scatter everything around. I ran as fast as I could but when I got to the front of the school building the turnaround was empty. The smell of exhaust hung in the air.

I dropped my stuff and sat down on the curb. How could I be so stupid? All I had to do was make it through the day and get on the bus and go home and I couldn't even do that. Instead I had let Budgie get to me again. I wished I could go back in time and do the day again only this time when Barely O'Donahue said, "Budgie climbed the tree," I'd say, "Good for him" or "Get bent" or something—*anything*—other than what I'd actually said. Sometimes I wished I could just take my brain out and put it in a box and bury it.

I went to wipe my dirty hands on my jeans but they

were just as bad if not worse. My shirt was dirty, too. I was scratched in a few places and bleeding. Mom was going to kill me if I ever got home. I could just see Budgie sitting in the back of the bus smiling and thinking he was so clever. Maybe if he smiled wide enough the top of his head would fall off.

I pictured him on all fours, feeling around for his head and getting all dirty and gross from the bus floor while everyone laughed and pointed at him for a change. Even though it didn't help me get home at all, picturing Budgie getting exactly what he deserved made me feel a little bit better.

"Derek?"

I looked over my shoulder at the lady standing behind me. I almost didn't recognize her but then I pictured her standing in front of a whiteboard.

"Ms. Dickson?"

"What are you doing here?" she asked.

"I missed the bus."

"Are you waiting for another one? Because there aren't any."

"No, I know, I—"

"What happened to your shirt?"

"My what? Nothing."

I couldn't tell her about the tree or I'd get in trouble and the last thing I needed right now was more of that. I was still on half recess for the whole bathroom thing. I tried to brush the bark dust off my shirt but only made it worse.

"I, um . . . fell down," I said, which, in a way, was true. I just didn't tell her how far I'd fallen.

Ms. Dickson didn't say anything. Was that it? I hoped that was it. I put my jacket on and zipped it up all the way. Maybe if she couldn't see my shirt she'd forget about it.

"Is someone coming to pick you up?"

"My aunt Josie doesn't have a car right now because she was in an accident and it's being fixed and my mom's at work."

"So no?"

"No."

"What are you going to do then, I wonder."

I thought about it for a minute and realized there wasn't much I *could* do. Calling Mom was out. Calling Aunt Josie was out, too, because she'd just turn around and call my mom anyway. Walking was out. It was too far. What else was there? Taxi? Jet pack? Hovercycle? I suddenly felt like I might throw up. I looked at Ms. Dickson and shrugged.

"Come along then," she said. "I'll take you home."

Ms. Dickson started to walk away toward the parking lot. I must have been hearing things because it had sounded like she said she'd take me home and that couldn't be right. I didn't even think that was possible. Budgie said that if teachers get too far away from school they blow up. I watched Ms. Dickson. She seemed okay. I couldn't hear ticking or anything.

"For pity's sake, Derek, stop dawdling!" she said.

I grabbed my bag and ran after her. The barfy feeling was gone and I felt lighter—like I could fly almost. Budgie's plan had backfired and I was going home and nobody would have to call anybody and nobody would get in trouble and as I got into the back of Ms. Dickson's car I swore I'd try to never let Budgie get to me again and this time I meant it.

Ms. Dickson's car was kinda like my mom's only it was clean and didn't smell like hot dogs. There weren't any soda cups on the floor or fish cracker crumbs in the seats. I got the feeling that there hadn't been any kids in Ms. Dickson's car in a long time.

"Where do you live?"

"In a house. Sorry. A *white* house."

"I meant what is your address?"

I told her but before she started the car she took out her cell phone, handed it to me, and asked me to call home and explain to Aunt Josie what was going on. Aunt Josie listened while I spoke. Then she spoke to Ms. Dickson. When Ms. Dickson was done she started the car and backed out of the parking space. She drove the car for a while and didn't say anything, which was fine with me. I figured it would be strange talking to her outside the classroom. I mean, I barely had anything to say when I was *in* the classroom so it wasn't like I would suddenly have all this stuff to talk about now that I was out of it.

"I taught your father, you know."

"What?"

"I was your father's English teacher when he was in the eighth grade," said Ms. Dickson. "We read *Catcher in the Rye* that year. Some of us did, anyway."

"My dad? Really?"

I had never really thought about what my dad was like when he was younger. I bet he was cool, though, like with slicked-back hair and a motorcycle. And sunglasses. I bet he had sunglasses. All cool guys had sunglasses.

"What was he like?"

"There are two students I remember very well from that year because it was my first year teaching in this district and Jason Lamb is one of them."

I smiled when Ms. Dickson said my dad's name because

I didn't hear it a lot. Mom always called him Bunny.

"Your father wasn't a great student. He wasn't a *bad* student, necessarily . . . just not a great one. The thing about your father, Derek, is that he always did his best. And no matter how bad the situation, no matter how frustrated he might get, he wouldn't let anything beat him. He was also a good *person*. He had a good *heart*. And in the end . . . well . . . let's just say that in the end we are judged not upon the strength of Holden Caulfield's character but upon our own."

"Was he the other guy?"

"What other guy?"

"You said you remembered two students from that year—my dad and some other guy. Was he the other guy? Was he a good person, too?"

"Holden Caulfield is the main character in one of the greatest works of American literature of the twentieth century," Ms. Dickson said. "Whereas Rory McReady threw his desk at me on more than one occasion."

"So Holden Caulfield wasn't the other guy."

"No."

It was weird listening to Ms. Dickson talk about stuff other than math or reading. It was weird that she knew my dad. It was weird that she *liked* my dad because I liked my dad, too, and let me tell you—having something in common with Ms. Dickson was the weirdest part of all.

"What's he doing these days?" she said.

I told her how my dad was far away in Afghanistan flying helicopters for the army and how it had been eight months, one week, and four days since he was home and how before that I hadn't seen him much since I was five. I also told her that the last time he came home he was supposed to stay home and we even had a big party with cake and two kinds of ice cream but then one day he got a letter in the mail and he had to go back.

Ms. Dickson got quiet all of a sudden and I sort of got the feeling she was frowning. Not like she was mad, though. It was more like she was sad or like she was thinking.

"Eight months, one week, and four days is a long time not to see your father."

"We write letters back and forth so it's not so bad," I said.

Ms. Dickson got quiet again and she stayed that way until we got to my house. She stopped the car and turned around in her seat and looked at me with a funny expression on her face like the one Mom gets when I'm sad or I've hurt myself. She looked at me like that for what seemed like a long time. It made me a little uncomfortable. I pulled my book bag into my lap.

"I hafta go now, Ms. Dickson," I said.

"Of course you do," she said.

"Thanks for the ride."

"You're welcome. Oh, and Derek?"

"Yes?"

"The next time you write your father could you tell him Ms. Dickson is thinking of him?"

Out of the corner of my eye I could see my aunt Josie standing on the front stoop. You can tell my mom and my aunt Josie are sisters because they look exactly the same when they're getting impatient.

"I really gotta go now. My aunt's waiting."

"What are you doing talking to me then? Shoo! Shoo!"

I got out of the car. I'd never heard Ms. Dickson talk like that—like a regular person, I mean. Usually no matter what she says she sounds like a teacher. I waved good-bye to her as she drove away.

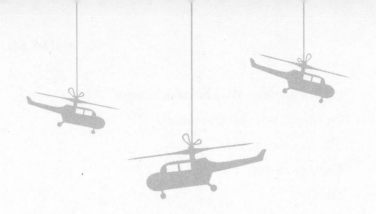

WE HAD OUR FIRST meeting for *A Christmas Carol* in the middle school cafeteria which meant I had to hoof it all the way from Ms. Dickson's classroom at the end of the fifth grade hallway to the other end of the school past the auditorium and along the hallway that connected the two buildings and I know that might not sound far but it was. Believe me.

Mr. Putnam was late and Violet and I had to listen to all the middle schoolers talk about middle school stuff, which, after a while, was really starting to terrify me. Dances? Permanent records? My mind whirled. I was pretty sure no one had even *tried* to tell us about those things. Violet and I sat there, not really looking at each other or saying anything. I was getting tired of listening to middle school stuff.

"Did you watch *Zeroman* last night?" I asked Violet.

"What's that?"

"*Zeroman*. You know. The TV show?"

"Oh. No."

"You probably watch *Jenny Rainbow and the Starlight Pony Squad*, right?"

"No."

"*A Dog Named Cat*?"

"No."

"What do you watch then?"

"Nothing."

"Cable out?"

"No."

"What's wrong with your TV?"

"Nothing," said Violet. "We don't have one."

She might have said more things after that but I stopped listening. I couldn't help it. Not seeing *Zeroman* was one thing, but not having a TV at all? What did her family do to pass the time—read? Talk to each other? It just didn't seem right. I was still wondering what Violet and her family did without a television when the cafeteria doors banged open and Mr. Putnam entered.

Everything about him was big. He was tall and wide and big around the middle. His voice was big. Even his beard was big. The air seemed to get out of his way when he moved. He sat at an empty table, cracked his knuckles, and opened his briefcase. He took out a bundle of papers and held it up.

"This, ladies and gentlemen, is a copy of the script," he boomed. "In time you will each have your own to work from but since I seem to have broken the copy machine, today we have six."

Some of the middle schoolers laughed. Mr. Putnam stroked his beard and cracked his knuckles again.

"Come, gather round, gather round," he said, waving us all to the table. "Most of you were probably too busy to notice but we are joined today by Monsieur Derek Lamb and Mademoiselle Violet Gardener from Ms. Dickson's fifth-grade class. Please join me in welcoming them."

My cheeks got hot and I put my head down a little. I was starting to wonder if this whole thing was a mistake when the strangest thing happened—Mr. Putnam and all of the middle schoolers stood up and *clapped their hands*!

A kid next to me who I'd never seen before even put his hand out so I could shake it. Some of the girls were giving Violet hugs and Violet had a big smile on her face and was hugging them back. Mr. Putnam thumped me on the back and I swear my skeleton almost jumped out. It was weird. I didn't think anyone had been that happy to meet me before.

That afternoon we did a read-through, which is where you just sit and read the script out loud for the first time. Me and Violet were in only one scene and it was a small one. It was the one where the Ghost of Christmas Past takes Scrooge back in time to when he was a little boy trapped alone in a schoolhouse on Christmas Eve and had to be rescued by his sister. I was going to be Young Scrooge, and as if being rescued by a girl wasn't bad enough, Young Scrooge is *so* happy that he *embraces* her. I had a pretty good idea of what embracing was but wasn't completely sure. I hoped it wasn't what I was thinking of.

"Trouble with the script, Mr. Lamb?"

Mr. Putnam was looking at me with a raised eyebrow. I'd noticed a lot of people had been looking at me like that lately.

"Um . . . embracing?"

"Yes?"

"That's like hugging, right?"

"Yes. Only more so."

So it *was* what I was thinking of. Great. Couldn't Young Scrooge and his sister fist-bump or high-five instead? Couldn't they just shake hands? What kind of weirdo hugged his sister, anyway? It didn't seem right. Violet and all the others were looking at me, waiting for me to do something.

"Right. Okay. Embracing. Got it."

"Are you sure?"

"Of course! I love embracing things. I'm like a professional embracer."

Mr. Putnam's eyebrow came down as the other one went up. I'd never seen that before. He stroked his beard and cracked his knuckles. There was a funny little grin on his face and I couldn't tell what he was thinking.

"Seriously," I said. "I'll embrace you right here."

He put up his hands.

"Easy, tiger," he said. "We hardly know each other."

Some of the middle schoolers laughed and Mr. Putnam was smiling and that's how I knew it was okay and they weren't being mean. He was just being funny. I sort of laughed a little then, too, even though I didn't really get it. After the read-through this kid named Desmond asked Mr. Putnam when the next practice would be and he said, "Desi, me boy . . . *jocks* practice. But actors, oh . . . actors *rehearse*!"

Mr. Putnam rolled the *r* the way Señora Cruz likes us to when we're doing Spanish. I couldn't do it right. Either I wouldn't roll the *r* enough or I'd roll it too much and end up spitting on someone by accident. Don't ask me how it happened but it did.

The rehearsal ended and I walked with Violet out to the front of the school and we sat on a bench by the turnaround. Mr. Putnam had given us a script to share and Violet had her nose in it, reading scenes we weren't even in. I'd also caught her paying attention during the read-through while I'd been trying unsuccessfully to solve her television problem.

"So what *do* you do?" I said.

"About what?"

"About not having a TV," I said. "I mean, how does that even happen?"

"My parents don't believe in it," said Violet. "They say it rots your brain."

"No way! That's what *my* mom says!"

"Is your mom a professor, too?"

"No, she's a nurse. Wait—are *both* your parents professors?"

"Yes."

"So is it like school all the time?"

"No," said Violet. "It's just normal."

"Well, not *normal*. I mean, you don't have a TV and TVs are pretty normal. Seriously, you can ask anybody."

A car pulled into the turnaround and the horn beeped twice.

"That's my dad, Derek, I gotta go," said Violet. "See you tomorrow."

Violet put the script in her book bag and stood up and walked to the car. She opened the door and got in. Before Violet could shut her door I shouted, "What do you do for fun? Flash cards?"

Only I wasn't teasing. I really wanted to know. Violet closed the door and waved as the car drove away. My mom's car pulled into the turnaround a few minutes later. I opened the door and got in and put my book bag on the seat next to me and buckled up.

"Hi, Mom," I said.

Only it wasn't Mom.

"Oh hey, Aunt Josie. Where's Mom?"

Aunt Josie looked at me in the rearview mirror. She was wearing her glasses with the black frames—her Clark Kent glasses as she called them. I'd put them on once to see how cool I looked but it was so blurry I could barely even see the mirror. Man, Aunt Josie was *blind*.

She started to say something but had to stop and clear her throat and start again. Her smile didn't look right. It looked on purpose.

"She's at home. She's, um . . . not feeling well, sweetie, and she asked me to come get you. Cool?"

"Can I ask you something?"

"You can ask me anything."

"If you didn't have a TV what would you do for fun?"

"I don't know. Paint, I guess. Cook? Why do you ask?"

I told her about Violet and about how her parents were professors and how they didn't have a TV.

"Do you think Violet cooks?" I asked.

"I don't know, Derek."

"I know she likes to read. What else do you think she does?"

"I don't know, Derek. I've never met her."

"Maybe she likes gardening."

"Maybe . . ."

"You think so?"

"Dude, I don't know her."

"She's Violet. From my class."

"Wanna listen to some music?" Aunt Josie said suddenly. "I've got some stuff in here you haven't heard yet."

She selected a CD and a track number and turned it up before I could answer. I looked out the window and wondered if Violet liked punk rock because I sure didn't. I tried not to listen and thought about who would win a fight between Hammerfist and Deathpunch instead.

I considered all the variables—individual martial arts expertise, Deathpunch's quickness versus Hammerfist's strength and mutant healing factor—I even broke down their training, upbringing, and dojo affiliation. It went back and forth and there still wasn't a clear winner by the time we got home.

My mom wasn't in the kitchen when we came in. She wasn't in the living room, either. She was in her bedroom with the lights off, all curled up on the bed. Aunt Josie went and sat next to her. I heard her whisper my mom's name a couple times and when she didn't answer Aunt Josie pulled the quilt from the foot of the bed and tucked it in around her so she wouldn't get cold. Then she came back out into the hallway and closed the door.

"Looks like it's just us for dinner," she said. "You up for some Pizza Jungle? You can have whatever toppings you want."

"Even jalapeños?"

Mom never let me get jalapeños because she said I wouldn't like them and it would be wasteful, which, of course, made me want them even more. I kinda figured it was now or never.

"*Half*," said Aunt Josie. "And I'll throw in an order of cheesy breadsticks."

"Extra dipping sauce?"

"Deal," she said, handing me the phone. "But you have to call and order it."

I called Pizza Jungle and ordered a large, half-jalapeño,

half-mushroom pizza and cheesy breadsticks with extra dipping sauce. Then I lay on the floor in the living room and did homework while Aunt Josie talked on the phone in the kitchen. When the guy from Pizza Jungle showed up she took the phone and left the room.

Pizza Jungle was my favorite because the delivery guys wore these funny gorilla masks and they had monkeys driving the delivery vans in the commercials. The pizza was pretty good, too. I paid for dinner with money Aunt Josie had left on the kitchen table and then got plates and glasses off the drying rack by the sink and milk from the fridge.

By the time Aunt Josie came to the table I'd already eaten most of the cheesy breadsticks and a slice of the jalapeño pizza. It was different from how I thought it would be. And not really in a good way. Aunt Josie sat down and picked up a slice of mushroom.

"Wanna try some jalapeño?"

"Why? Don't you like it?" she said.

"What? No, it's great! It's awesome!" I said. "Just . . . you should have some before I eat it all."

"No thanks."

"You're sure?"

"Derek, I'm crashing on the pull-out couch tonight, cool?"

Usually it was great when Aunt Josie stayed over because in the morning she would make this kind of French toast that's all crunchy on the outside, but something told me that this time there wouldn't be any. It didn't seem like it was going to be that kind of visit. She had a bite of her pizza and put the slice back in the box and closed the lid.

"Guess I wasn't as hungry as I thought I was," she said.

"Yeah, me too."

"Derek?"

"Yeah?"

"You can pick the peppers off if you want to. It's okay if you don't like them."

"No, I like them! I just . . . I feel a little bit full."

"Derek."

"I don't like them," I said. "They made my head sweat so much I thought I was melting."

"Wow. That's hot."

"Yeah, it was like biting into the *sun*!"

"No way!"

"Yes way," I said. "Can I be excused?"

"Did you get enough to eat?"

"Yeah."

"What about veggies?"

"What?"

"Did you get any veggies?"

"Jalapeños are veggies," I said. "And the dipping sauce is made from tomatoes."

After I'd cleared my plate and put the pizza box in the fridge I went into the living room and found the remote and turned on the TV. *Zeroman* was going to be on soon. It was the episode where Zeroman is captured by the evil Dr. Mayhem, who has built a mind-switching machine and plans to switch minds with Zeroman so he can get close to the president, capture him, and then switch minds with *him* and take over the world. I'd only seen the episode four times before, though, so I was a little fuzzy on the details.

It was the end of the commercials and *Zeroman* was supposed to be on next but instead of the opening part with the theme music it showed an American flag being lowered with the White House in the background. I thought maybe I'd switched to a news channel or something by accident but the remote was right where I'd left it on the arm of the couch.

On TV the American flag was gone and a black one was being raised in its place and when it got to the top of the pole the wind snapped it open, revealing a clenched fist with lightning bolts coming out of it. My jaw dropped. The dreaded Mayhem symbol! The words *coming soon* appeared in the middle of the screen and the sound of Dr. Mayhem's laughter rang in my head long after they'd returned to the regularly scheduled *Zeroman* episode.

Later that night I lay in bed staring up at the Apache helicopter, too excited to sleep. Had Dr. Mayhem's nefarious plot finally succeeded? Where was Zeroman? Coming soon? How soon? Suddenly nothing else seemed important. Everything fell away—homework, play rehearsal, Budgie—those things just didn't matter anymore. There was only the mystery of what had happened. I didn't think I'd think about anything else ever again.

I'd thought about it while I brushed my teeth and put my pajamas on and I'd thought about it as I got in bed. I thought about it for hours and hours and the only thing I could say for sure was that it was totally unfair for the TV people to make me wait. In fact, the whole thing seemed downright mean. I stared up at the Apache helicopter and tried not to think about it.

Me and Dad are buzzing over a thick, green jungle toward a line of red smoke coming up out of the trees. My code name is Cochise. I'm wearing a cowboy hat that has an eagle feather in the hatband.

"There's the LZ, Cochise," Dad says, pointing out the

landing zone. "Looks like we'll have those POWs home in time for milk and cookies."

We buzz over to where the clearing should be but there isn't one. The smoke is rising from the tiniest of tiny breaks in the leaves.

"Something's not right," Dad says. "There should be a clearing here! Where's the clearing, Cochise?"

"I don't know!"

"I don't like this, man, not one bit."

"Me neither, Padre," I say. "Let's get the heck outta Dodge."

I'm turning the chopper around when the rocket blows off our tail rotors, sending us spinning out of control. Dad is shouting as we fall. I move the stick back and forth but nothing happens—without the tail rotors I may as well be trying to steer a tornado. I don't think either of us hears the second rocket.

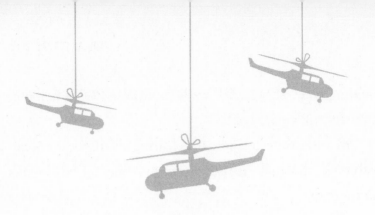

"THEN I WOKE UP. Isn't that a weird dream?"

It was morning and I was eating cereal at the kitchen table. Aunt Josie was drinking coffee. Actually, she was more like holding the coffee mug in her hands and staring at it. Her eyes had these dark circles under them. Mom was still sleeping.

"Aunt Josie?"

"Hm?" she said. "Oh! You're right, that *is* a weird dream."

"What did you dream about?"

"I don't remember. I didn't sleep very well last night, sweetie."

"Why not?"

"Um . . . the pull-out couch hurts my back."

"Is that why you're so sad this morning?"

She nodded her head. "Yeah."

I picked up my empty cereal bowl and went and put it in the sink. I even ran water into it like Mom always asks.

Then I went upstairs and brushed my teeth and came back down and put my shoes and jacket on. Aunt Josie was still sitting at the kitchen table. I went over to her and gave her a big hug.

"I hope you feel better."

"Thanks, Derek," she said. "Have a good day at school and I'll see you this afternoon."

"Why? Is Mom working another late shift?"

"No."

"Then why—?"

"You're going to miss the bus if you don't go now, okay?"

"But what about my lunch? Mom usually makes me lunch."

"You'll just have buy lunch today. Get my purse for me?"

I brought it to her and she got her wallet out and looked in it. She took out a bill and handed to me. It had the number ten on it. It had to be a mistake. I looked at Aunt Josie. Aunt Josie looked at me.

"It's all I have," she said.

"But it's a ten."

"Just keep it."

"Really?"

"Yes."

"I can keep it?"

"Yes."

"Really?"

"You're going to miss the bus."

"Woo-hoo! I'm rich!" I held the bill up to my face and squinted so I could read the tiny letters. "Helloooo President Hamilton!"

Budgie wasn't at the bus stop when I got there. Also Aunt Josie had forgotten to remind me to wear a hat and my head was cold. Maybe there would be enough money left after I bought lunch to buy one.

A car pulled up to the bus stop that wasn't Budgie's mom's minivan or Budgie's dad's big, silver spy car. It was small and blue with two doors and one of them opened and I was surprised to see Budgie get out. He walked over to me as the blue car drove away. When it was gone Budgie stuck a finger in the air but if he was trying to do a peace sign he was only getting it half-right.

"Who was that?"

"Her name's Phoebe," grumbled Budgie.

"Who's Phoebe?"

Budgie mumbled something and shoved his hands into his pockets and kinda turned away.

"What?"

"*Nanny*, okay? She's my—my parents got me a nanny."

"A nanny? Why?"

"I don't know! It's—I—shut up, Lamb! Just shut up!"

He got right in my face and poked a finger in my chest. "If you tell anyone about this I'll punch you in the wiener so hard it'll come out your butt!"

I told him that his secret was safe with me but by the time recess rolled around just about everybody knew, which was weird because I'd only told two or three kids and I made them swear they wouldn't tell anyone. I didn't see what the big deal was, anyway. As far as I could tell, a nanny was just one more person to play with.

We didn't get to go outside for recess because it was too cold and it had started to rain. I was at my desk drawing a picture of a giant robot fighting a T. rex when Barely O'Donahue walked by and bumped my desk on purpose so I'd mess up.

"Dude!"

"Budgie says he's gonna punch you in the wiener because you told everyone about his nanny."

"No I didn't."

"Yes you did."

"I didn't tell you, did I?"

"No but—"

"Then how do you know?"

"Budgie told me."

"Wow," I said. "Big secret."

Barely O'Donahue walked away and I went back to drawing. I was able to turn the mess-up he caused into a laser sword for the T. rex, which was actually pretty cool. I wasn't that worried about Budgie punching me in the wiener because he'd have to sneak up on me to do it and I didn't think he could. The universe had rules, after all. For example, two things couldn't be in the same place at the same time, and there's no such thing as a fat ninja.

Then, during reading block, it happened. Missy Sprout was reading out loud from a book and I didn't have to listen to know it was about horses because books about horses are the only kind she reads. She may have read about unicorns once or twice but she wasn't fooling anybody.

"Budgie!" said Ms. Dickson.

"What? I'm not doing anything," said Budgie.

"Give me the note."

"What note?"

"The note, Budgie," said Ms. Dickson. "The one you were handing to Sally. Bring it to me, please."

Everybody watched Budgie walk up and put a folded-up piece of paper in Ms. Dickson's hand. Then he stood there with his back to the classroom and his head down.

His ears had gone red. Ms. Dickson opened the note and read it to herself. Then she folded it up again and put it on her desk. She got a dry erase marker, went to the board, and wrote *weener* in big letters.

The boys all cracked up. Even some of the girls laughed, too. Missy Sprout just looked upset because she had to stop reading about horses for five seconds. Budgie made fists with his hands and I was pretty sure that if his ears got any redder they'd burst into flame. I bet he was wishing the floor would open up and swallow him whole. I knew that feeling. It wasn't fun. I kinda felt bad for him.

"Can anyone tell me the correct spelling of this word?"

"Wiener," said Violet. It was funny to hear a girl say it. "W-I-E-N-E-R. Wiener."

Ms. Dickson wrote the right spelling on the board and then handed the marker to Budgie.

"Please copy this word twenty-five times using the correct spelling, please."

Budgie didn't say anything. He just went to the board and started copying while most of the class laughed. Missy Sprout wasn't laughing. And this time I wasn't, either.

Mom was up when I got home. She was in her bathrobe, drinking tea at the kitchen table with Aunt Josie. Her hair was back and I could tell she'd been crying because her eyes were puffy and a little bit red.

"Mom!"

I ran over and gave her a big hug. I put my face against her neck the way I used to when I was little and closed my eyes tight. She hugged me back and put her fingers in my hair. We squeezed and squeezed.

"Piggy, did you wear a hat today?"

"I kinda forgot," I said. "But Aunt Josie didn't—"

"Don't blame Aunt Josie when it's your job to remember. I'm just glad you didn't lose another hat."

"Come on, that only happened that one . . ." I stopped and thought for a second. "Those two—three times."

"Derek, you know hats cost money," Mom said. "And money doesn't grow on trees."

"I know," I said. "Same as hot dogs."

"Hot dogs?" said Aunt Josie.

"When Derek was four he planted a cocktail wienie in the backyard because he thought it was a hot dog seed."

This one time at lunch, a kid named Rufus Hornblower laughed so hard that milk came out his nose. I didn't know it could happen with tea. I don't think Aunt Josie knew it either because she looked *really* surprised. She put her mug down quickly and grabbed a bunch of napkins and wiped her face and the front of her shirt.

"Oh my God! That's—why am I just hearing about this now?"

"I never told you?" said Mom. She smiled and even laughed a little.

"No. I would have remembered that. Be*lieve* me."

I smiled, too, and not just because Mom did but also because it was pretty hilarious seeing Aunt Josie shoot tea out of her nose. It was almost as funny as the time a couple weeks ago when Budgie dropped the dry erase marker at the board and split his pants bending over to get it. And if that hadn't been enough, Ms. Dickson made him stand in the supply closet in his underwear while she fixed his pants with a stapler.

"What? I thought I could grow a hot dog tree," I said. Then from over Mom's shoulder I noticed the garbage can was out and it was full of broken stuff. "What happened to all the dishes?"

Aunt Josie looked at Mom. Then she looked at me.

"It was an accident," she said. "I was emptying the dish-washer and—"

"But they're like . . . *all* broken."

"It was an accident," said Mom in a tiny voice I barely heard.

She didn't say anything after that. Aunt Josie didn't say anything either but she reached over and put her hand on

Mom's arm. It was quiet for what seemed like a really long time. Then Mom closed her eyes and took a deep breath and let it out slowly. When she opened them they were wet. She looked at Aunt Josie for a second and then back at me.

"Derek . . . your father . . ."

"Will he be home for Christmas?"

The words just came out. I'd learned not to hope too much for Dad to be home for birthdays or Thanksgivings or things like that because when I did, I always ended up disappointed, but he hadn't been here for Christmas since I was five and this time I was in a play and everything. It was like if he could just be here for this Christmas I could forget all of the other stuff.

Mom shook her head and closed her eyes tight but tears came out anyway. She wiped them off and cleared her throat and looked at me.

"I don't think so," she said, hugging me so tight I almost couldn't breathe. Her whole body was shaking.

"But maybe?"

"Your father is . . . he's . . ."

"What's wrong?"

"I, um . . . nothing." She shook her head. "I just really miss him. That's all."

"I miss him, too," I said. "Hey, can I tell you something?"

"You can tell me anything, Piglet."

"There's gonna be a special episode of *Zeroman* soon where Dr. Mayhem finally takes over the world only it's longer than a regular episode and it's on past my bedtime but can I please stay up and watch it, please?"

"I don't know, Derek. Can you ask me again later?"

"Yeah. Oh and also? Can you let me go now because I really hafta go pee and your squeezing is kinda making it come out a little."

She let me go and I took off for the bathroom. I had to go so bad I didn't even take time to close the door even though Mom says it's rude to go with it open. I'm usually pretty good about it but this time it was an emergency and I figured she'd rather I get to the toilet instead of going in my pants. When I was done I washed my hands and went back to the kitchen where I found Aunt Josie rinsing out the mugs.

"Where'd Mom go?"

"Upstairs to lie down."

"Is she okay?"

Aunt Josie shrugged but didn't turn around. She kept on rinsing out the mugs, running them back and forth under the water. They must have been really dirty.

"No," she said. "Not really."

"Is she sick?"

"She's sad."

"Why is she sad? Did I do something?"

I'd been pretty good lately. I mean there was the hat thing from this morning but I didn't think that was it. And she hadn't seen me peeing with the door open, either, and those were really the only two things I could think of.

"And also? Aunt Josie? Y'know you don't need to wash out those mugs. You can just put those in the dishwasher."

"I know that. I just need . . ." She turned from the sink and looked at me. Her hands were bright red from being under the hot water. They looked angry. "Why don't you run up and do some homework before dinner, okay?"

"But it's Friday. I don't do homework on Fridays," I said. "And besides, I didn't even get a snack."

"So get one."

"Won't that ruin my appetite?"

"I don't know, Derek, will it?"

"Probably."

"Well there you go, then."

"But I'm a little bit hungry."

"Then get a snack! For Christ's sake, what do you want me to tell you?"

But I didn't get a snack. I ran up to my room and slammed the door and locked it even though I wasn't supposed to. I didn't even care if the lock broke and I couldn't get out. I almost *wanted* the lock to break. That way I'd be stuck in there and probably die of starvation and it would be all Aunt Josie's fault for yelling at me.

I lay down on my bed. I could hear Aunt Josie calling my name from the bottom of the stairs but I didn't answer her. I went and got my desk chair and stuck it under the doorknob instead. Then I went back to my bed and lay down again and stared at the ceiling. I looked up at the Apache helicopter and thought about my dad. He wouldn't have yelled at me like that.

I got off the bed and reached under and felt around until I found it—an old plastic lunchbox that had a cool, black car on it with *Knight Rider* written underneath. It had belonged to my dad when he was my age and was filled with every letter he'd ever written me. I opened it and counted them out until there were ninety-one arranged on my quilt. I found the very first one and picked it up and opened it.

> *Derek,*
>   *Hello from Fort Benning!*
>   *First of all—thank you for your letter. It was such a nice surprise! Please write me as much as you want, kiddo, I love hearing about what you're doing.*

To answer your questions,

Yes—basic training (BCT) is hard work. We wake up at 0500 (5:00 a.m.) and our bedtime is 2130 (9:30 p.m.). In between we do a lot of running, marching, shouting, and push-ups. It is VERY important to listen and follow directions— just like it is for you at school. We have classes, too, so it's kind of like we're going to school together. Pretty cool, huh?

No—I don't have my own bedroom. Instead, I sleep in a very big room with 49 other recruits who are all different ages and come from different backgrounds from all over the country. The guy in the rack (bed) to my right is an 18-year-old from a small town in West Virginia that only has 20 people in it! The recruit on my other side is also 18 but lives in New York City where he is one of millions! Yes—we have been given guns but we have not fired them yet. We are learning how to take care of them first. We take them apart, clean them, and put them back together again and again. They also don't call them guns. They call them rifles. So from now on I will too.

What else can I tell you?

It's very hot here. There's a lot of sand and a

lot, LOT of fire ants. Whenever anyone drops a
tray in the mess hall (dining room) everyone yells
AIRBORNE! It really startled me the first time it
happened.

I miss you and Mom very, very much and I
think about you all the time. I have to go now, it's
almost lights out (bedtime). I'll write every chance
I get and you write me, OK?
I LOVE YOU,
Pvt. Dad

I read it again and when I'd finished, it felt like there
was something stuck in my throat. I swallowed but it
wouldn't go away. I put the letter back in the envelope and
the envelope back in the lunch box. Then I picked up the
rest of the letters one by one and put them away, too, closing
the lid and putting the lunch box back under the bed when
I was done. Then I just sat on the floor feeling weird and
hollow—almost like I wasn't even there.

I got my chair from under the doorknob and took it to
my desk where I got out some paper and a pencil.

Dear Dad,
Hi, how are you? I am fine. School was good
today. Can you come home now? That way you

would be here for Christmas and you could see me in the play. Mom really misses you and the foldout couch hurts Ant Josie's back. I'll get some tools and fix it. Maybe that will make her less cranky. Do you remember Ms. Dickson? She remembers you.

I remember you too.

Love,
DEREK

I got an envelope from the drawer and folded up the letter and put it in. Then I sealed it with Scotch tape because I hated licking the glue. I carefully wrote the address on the front and then used my special ink pad and stamp that said "Master Derek Lamb" on it for the return address because it looked more official and Dad would know I wasn't fooling around.

A knock at the door made me jump.

"Derek?"

It was Aunt Josie. I didn't say anything because I was still kinda mad. She knocked again only this time it was louder. I still didn't say anything. It didn't feel right not answering her, though. It felt rude and a little bit mean.

"Derek, sweetie? I'm sorry I barked at you."

· "You didn't bark at me."

"Yes, I did and I'm sorry."

"That's okay."

"No, it's not."

"Um . . . thank you for saying sorry?"

"You're welcome," she said.

It was quiet for a minute after that. I could picture her in the hallway with one hand on the door, thinking of what to say next.

"Derek?"

"Yes?"

"Can I come in?"

I got up from my chair and went to the door and opened it. Aunt Josie came in and bent down and gave me a hug. She squeezed me tight and her hair tickled my nose. It was blonde this time. So blonde it was almost white.

"You're my boo and I want you to know that I'll be here for you no matter what."

"Okay."

Aunt Josie put her hands on my shoulders, looked me right in the eyes, and brushed the hair out of my face with her fingers. Her face was serious.

"Honestly," she said. "No. Matter. What."

"Right. Gotcha."

I nodded, hoping she'd let me go because I could smell garlic bread and garlic bread meant spaghetti and spaghetti was just about my favorite food in the whole universe. My stomach growled.

"What was that?"

"My stomach," I said.

"*That* was your *stomach*?"

"Uh-huh."

"You're not hiding a lion under your bed?"

"It was my stomach."

"Then we'd better put some food in it before it escapes and eats us all."

I pictured my stomach bursting out of my body. It was all pink and red and slimy and had little arms and legs and a big mouth full of fangs. I imagined it chasing Budgie down the street, snapping at his ankles and growling all the way.

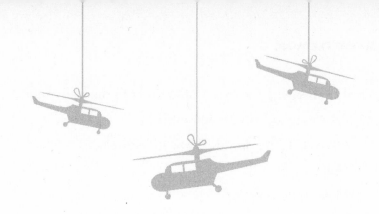

THE SMELL OF COFFEE woke me up. I reached over and lifted the blind a little and peeked out. The sun was just starting to come up and the world outside the window was full of shadows. I got out of bed and went to my closet and got my slippers and a hoodie sweatshirt and went downstairs to the kitchen.

Mom stood at the counter waiting for the coffee-maker to beep. She was wearing her purple robe and a pair of Dad's slippers. Her hair was wild. I think she may have still been asleep, which would have been something because you could totally hear Aunt Josie snoring in the other room and it was pretty loud.

"Hey, Mom!"

"Hm?"

Mom looked over at me. Her eyes were half-shut and there were dark circles under them.

"Oh! Hi, Piggy. How'd you sleep?"

Her voice was all mumbly but I knew what she said.

She'd been saying the exact same thing to me every morning for as long as I could remember.

"Okay, I think," I said. "How did you sleep?"

"Hm?"

"How did *you* sleep?"

"Not well, sweetie. Not well at all."

"Maybe you could take a nap later," I said.

She smiled a little—the kind where it's not really a smile at all.

"Maybe."

The coffeemaker beeped and Mom got a mug from the drying rack and poured coffee into it. She took it to the table and sat down. I stood there in my slippers and sweatshirt and waited for something else to happen. When it didn't I grabbed the last of the frozen waffles from the freezer and stuck them in the toaster oven and turned it on.

"Breakfast! You need breakfast," Mom exclaimed suddenly. She got up out of her chair so fast she almost spilled her coffee. "I can't believe I forgot! I'm the worst mother in the world."

"I don't know, Mom. The world's a pretty big place."

"Here, what can I get for you? Waffles? Let me get you some waffles."

She opened the freezer and moved some things around. A bag of frozen chicken nuggets fell out and landed on her foot.

"Dammit! I'm so sorry about this, honey. It's just . . . I've been—where the hell are the waffles already?"

"They're in the toaster. Mom, it's okay."

"It's not," she said. "It's really not."

"They're just waffles."

"Annie? What's going on?" Aunt Josie stood in the doorway, yawning and rubbing her eyes.

Mom picked up the bag of chicken nuggets and put it back in the freezer and shut the door. Then she leaned her forehead against it and closed her eyes.

"I forgot to fix breakfast for Derek," she said.

"Come on. Come sit down. Have some coffee," said Aunt Josie.

She took Mom's arm and sat her down and put the coffee in front of her. Then she sat down also. She looked worried. I wondered if there might be something else going on besides waffles but I didn't know what it was and I didn't think it was a good time to ask. Instead I got a plate from the cabinet and when my waffles were ready I put peanut butter and Marshmallow Fluff on them and took them into the living room to eat in front of cartoons. A little while later I thought I heard my mom cry out. A little while after that I smelled bacon.

Mom came in while I was watching *Dinoboy*. She took the quilt from the back of the couch and unfolded it so it covered both of us. Then she curled up against me with her head on my shoulder and we watched TV for a few minutes like that without saying anything.

"Dinoboy, eh?"

"Yup."

"And what does he do?"

"Oh, Mom, Dinoboy's so cool! He's this kid who can transform into any dinosaur! He can even be like part one kind and part another like a pterodactyl with the claws of a Therazinosaurus! Plus, did you know the Therazinosaurus was actually an herbivore? He used his claws to pull the leaves down from the trees and for self-defense. I think the Therazinosaurus is my favorite dinosaur or maybe the Compsognathus. He was only the size of a chicken! What's your favorite dinosaur, Mom? Mom?"

But she was asleep so I ended up watching the rest of *Dinoboy* with her leaned up against me. She got heavy after a while and I couldn't really feel my arm anymore but I was afraid to move it because I didn't want to wake her and it wasn't until a rerun of *Ghost Patrol* that she kinda rolled over a little and I was able to get out.

The rest of the morning went by okay. I went to my room and read comics for a while and then I got dressed and put on my jacket and played outside until I got cold. Mom was just getting off the phone when I came into the kitchen.

"Around 1:30 then? And you're sure it's okay?" she asked. "Great! Thanks, Helen!"

I didn't like the sound of that. Helen was Budgie's mom's name.

"Mom?"

"Hey, Piggy! Hungry for lunch?"

She got bread from the drawer and then opened the fridge and found some ham and cheese and mustard and took them out and put them all on the counter. Then she squirted a blob of mustard on a slice of bread and spread it around with a knife.

"Could you do me a favor and smell the ham?" she asked.

"Smell the—why?"

"To make sure it's still good. Oh, never mind. I'll do it."

She took a slice and held it to her nose and made a face. Then she sniffed it again, shrugged, and put it down on the bread.

"Who was that on the phone?" I asked.

"Budgie's mom," she said. "And listen, before you freak

out—I'm going out with your aunt Josie this afternoon. I called Budgie's mom to see if it would be okay if you went over there to play for a while."

My heart tumbled into my stomach. Play with Budgie? Budgie? The Dr. Mayhem to my Zeroman? Was she out of her mind?

"You want me to play with Budgie?"

"Yes."

"But he's my nemesis!"

"No, he's not. You're too young to have a nemesis."

"He's *mean* to me!"

"I know, Piggy, I'm sorry," she said. "You two used to get along so well, though. What happened?"

"I don't know. Now he's only nice to me when there's nobody else around and even then he's not *that* nice. He's just . . . less mean."

It was true. Budgie and I used to be friends. Actually, the summer his family moved to town I was the only friend he had. We did everything together—we made up these awesome superheroes, Strong Guy and Fast Guy, and ran around fighting the Forces of Evil. We read comics and played video games and watched *Dinoboy* together. We made up secret handshakes and were going to build a castle together and keep all the grown-ups out. It was going to be awesome.

Then when school started he met all these other kids and we didn't play together as much. Now we don't play at all. Now he doesn't like me and I don't know why. I've never even done anything to him. He even said that *Dinoboy* was for nerds.

"I'm sorry, sweetie," Mom said. "I absolutely *hate* that he's mean to you but it would just be the two of you. It's only for a little while, okay? Mommy really needs to get out of the house. Please?"

"Can I come with you?"

"No, honey, you can't. I'm sorry."

"Please?"

"Sorry."

"Please!"

"Raising your voice won't change anything," Mom said. "Now eat your lunch so we can get ready to go."

I took the sandwich and stomped over to the table. If I was a cartoon I'd have a big, black cloud over my head with lightning coming out of it. That's how mad I was. Mom put away the ham and cheese and mustard and then stood there and watched me eat. I put the hood of my sweatshirt up.

"Stop looking at me," I said.

"But you're so handsome."

"Stop it."

"But I love you."

"Mo-om!"

"Okay, okay," she said. "Want some chips?"

"Yes, please."

Mom got the potato chips from the cupboard and shook some onto my plate. I took the top slice of bread off the sandwich and put the chips on the inside. Then I replaced the bread and took a bite. A lot of sandwiches taste better with potato chips in them. Especially boring sandwiches like ham and cheese. Mom sat down across from me.

"Have you told him to stop?" Mom asked.

"Told who to stop what?"

"Budgie. To stop being mean."

"Yes. No. Not exactly," I said. "Even when I do tell him to stop he doesn't."

Mom put her hand on my arm and looked me in the eyes. She frowned.

"I'm sorry your friend is such a jerk, sweetie."

"Me too."

It was weird, though, because that afternoon at his house Budgie wasn't a jerk at all. Actually, it was just like it used to be. We played video games and drew some pictures for the Strong Guy and Fast Guy comic we were going to make. We even talked about plans for the castle. Budgie thought there should be piranhas in the moat and I thought crocodiles would be better so we invented a creature called a piranhadile and figured we'd stock the moat with a few of those bad boys.

We started up Derek and Budgie's Secret Secret Club again and made up a tricky new handshake that took five minutes to do. Then we hung a blanket from the top bunk so it made a fort of the bottom one. We got inside and held the new club's first official meeting where Budgie told me that one time he peed himself at school and tried to hide it by splashing water on his pants and telling everyone the water fountain was broken and had squirted him. I told him about the play and how I had to embrace Violet and how it actually wasn't as bad as I had thought it was going to be. I had been hanging on to that one and it felt good to finally tell someone. We sat quiet for a minute.

"So are you boyfriend and girlfriend?" Budgie finally asked.

"No. I don't know. I don't think so. Maybe."

"Do you think you'll get married?"

"Probably. Yeah."

"Y'wanna know something else weird?" I asked.

"Sure," said Budgie.

"On Fridays her hair smells like apples."

"What does it smell like on other days?"

"I don't know. Not apples."

"I don't know what's weirder," Budgie said. "The fact that her hair only smells like apples on Fridays or that you've taken the time to figure that out."

We talked about other stuff too for a while—the land-speed capabilities of zombies as affected by stage of decay, for example—and by the time Mom came to pick me up I didn't want to leave.

"Mrs. Lamb, can Derek sleep over?"

"Yeah, Mom, can I?"

"Some other time."

"But—"

"What would you sleep in? You don't even have a toothbrush."

"I'll use my finger! Please?"

"Yeah, and he can borrow some of my pajamas," said Budgie.

"It's not a good idea," Mom said. "Not tonight. Not on such short notice. I'm sure Budgie's mom—"

"She doesn't care," said Budgie.

"I suppose it would be okay," said Budgie's mom.

"You're so nice to offer, Helen, but I don't want to impose any more than I already have. Another time, maybe?"

Budgie's mom just stood there with her arms crossed

looking at us. She was kinda smiling but not really.

"Of course."

"Derek, say thank you," Mom said.

"What about tomorrow night?" said Budgie.

"Yeah, tomorrow night."

"Tomorrow's a school night," said my mom and Budgie's mom at the same time.

"Jinx!" said me and Budgie.

"Double jinx!" we said again.

"Derek, say thank you to Mrs. Pratt."

"Thank you, Mrs. Pratt," I said. "Bye, Budgie."

"Yeah, bye," he said. Then he turned around and went back upstairs.

"Thanks again for looking after Derek," Mom said. "If there's anything you need, if we could ever . . . you know."

"Of course," said Budgie's mom. "Careful on the walk, now. Some of the stones are loose."

We had leftover spaghetti for dinner that night, which was totally fine with me even though there wasn't any garlic bread left and we had to have regular bread instead. After dinner I went up to my room and bounced around for a little while, pretending I was Fast Guy fighting crime. Then I drew a picture of the castle me and Budgie were going to build and the moat with a piranhadile in it. The castle was big and had towers that had these little windows you could shoot arrows out of. There was also a roller coaster and a half-pipe for skateboarding. I didn't know how to skateboard and neither did Budgie but I figured by the time we got the castle built we probably would have learned.

I was putting the final touches on the castle when Mom came in. She stood behind me for a minute, looking over my shoulder at the drawing. I had to say it was pretty cool. I'd outdone myself with this one.

"Piranhagator?"

"Piranha*dile*."

"Silly me," she said. "Hey, do you have any interest in bathing tonight?"

"Why, am I stinky?"

"You've been worse," she said. "What are those?"

"Bumper cars."

"Very nice, Piggy. I think you've outdone yourself here."

"That's what *I* thought!"

"You know what, though, I need for you to get your pajamas on and get ready for bed, okay? And if you're not going to shower you should at least wash your face. And really brush your teeth. Chewing on the toothbrush doesn't count."

"But the toothpaste stings my tongue!"

"No, it doesn't."

"Yes, it does!"

"Derek, I don't know what to tell you," Mom said. "Life can sting sometimes."

"Like a bee?"

"Yes."

"Or a jellyfish?"

"Yes, like a jellyfish."

"A box jellyfish or a man o' war?"

"What's the difference?"

"Well, a box jellyfish is deadlier even though they both have poison tentacles. And the man o' war goes with the current and kinda floats but the box jellyfish can actually swim a little."

Mom looked at me and blinked a couple times. Her eyes seemed greener than normal. I smiled and nodded.

"Just brush your teeth, wise guy," she said. "And hop to, okay? It's almost bedtime."

"Can I finish the drawing?"

"Jammies and teeth first."

"But Mom—"

"Let me finish," she said. "Get into your pajamas and brush your teeth now and you can stay up an extra half-hour to finish the drawing or read or whatever, sound good?"

"Can I watch TV?"

"No."

"Why not?"

"Because I'd rather you used your brain."

I told her I'd been using my brain all day. I told her it was impossible to build forts, draw comics and castles, and create piranhadiles without it and that it might actually appreciate a rest. She said I made a great point and that she was proud of me for being so articulate. I wasn't sure what that meant but I didn't want to say anything. Sometimes if you do something good by accident it's best if you just pretend you meant to do it all along. You can always go back and figure out what it was later on.

"So can I stay up?"

"Aren't you tired from playing with Budgie all afternoon?"

"No."

"Pajamas and teeth first," said Mom. "Then it's okay."

I said thanks and gave her a big hug and then put on my pajamas and brushed my teeth and ran downstairs and turned on the TV just as *Zeroman* was starting. It was the one where Dr. Mayhem collects all these artifacts from all over the world that create a doomsday device when put together. There's this awesome part where Zeroman fights some sharks but can't use his knife or speargun because if

he cuts the sharks it would start a feeding frenzy so he has
to use underwater kung fu instead.

During the commercials I tried to remember the word
Mom used when she said was proud of me. If I could remember that, I could figure out what it meant and then be
like that all the time and get to stay up and watch TV. I was
still trying to remember the word a half-hour later as I got
into bed and a half-hour after that when I finally fell asleep.

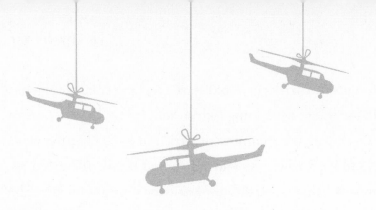

THE NEXT DAY no one picked up the phone over at Budgie's even though I really wanted to play again. I had thought of some more cool things for the castle and it was important that I talk to Budgie about them. I must have called fifteen times.

"Aunt Josie," I shouted from the top of the stairs. "There's something wrong with the phone!"

"Don't yell across the house, Derek," she shouted back. "Come down here if you want to talk to me."

I found Aunt Josie in the living room. She was sitting on the couch digging through the backpack in her lap and from where I stood I could see the little cartoon skull and crossbones tattooed behind her ear. Her big leopard-print suitcase stood in the corner.

"What're you looking for?" I asked.

"My toothbrush," said Aunt Josie. "I could've sworn . . ."

"Are you staying over?"

"I thought I'd come hang with you guys for a while if

that's okay with you," she said, smiling. A pair of sunglasses held her hair away from her face. It was red today. Like a fire engine.

"Heck yeah, it is," I said, holding out my fist. "Bump it. C'mon now, don't leave me hanging."

We bumped fists and blew it up. Aunt Josie was the coolest.

"Can you tattoo me?"

"Of course," she said, putting her backpack on the floor. "Run and get your markers, okay?"

I got the markers, sat down on the couch, and gave Aunt Josie my arm. She pushed my sleeve up over my elbow.

"Now what are we thinking of doing here?"

"You choose," I said. "But it has to be cool."

"When has it ever *not* been cool?"

I shook my head and closed my eyes. I could hear Aunt Josie open the box of markers and slide a few out. I wondered what colors she'd chosen.

"Why are you closing your eyes?"

"I don't want to see it until it's done," I said. "I want to be surprised."

"Suit yourself," said Aunt Josie. "Remember our motto?"

"Sit down. Shut up. And don't move."

"Attaboy!"

I closed my eyes a little tighter and clenched my teeth, waiting for the first stroke of the marker. Aunt Josie had a light hand and it always, *always* tickled at first—especially on the inside of the arm—but after the first few minutes you got used to it. She drew in silence for a while, holding my wrist loosely in one hand. I had no idea what she was drawing—footprints, maybe? It felt like they could be footprints.

"So how are things with your lady friend?" she asked suddenly.

"What lady friend?"

"You were telling me about her the other day. She has a flower name—Rose? Lily?"

"Oh, you mean Violet."

"That's it," said Aunt Josie. "And how is Violet?"

"Fine. I guess. Why?"

"You a little sweet on her, maybe?"

My face flushed and I almost opened my eyes.

"No. I don't—I'm not . . . no."

"You're sure?"

"Yes. No. Wait—if I'm sweet on her does that mean I like her?"

"Yes."

"Then no. I mean, yeah. I mean I'm not *in* like with her or anything. She's nice to me."

"Derek?"

"Yeah?"

"You're blushing."

"I know."

"Like crazy."

I didn't say anything. Instead, I tried flexing different facial muscles so I would get unblushed but I don't think it worked because my face and my neck and the room and the rest of the world still felt hot.

"I'm just messing with you, kiddo. It's perfectly normal if you like her," said Aunt Josie. "But I can't promise I won't get jealous. And y'know what?"

"What?"

"I think we're done here."

"I can open my eyes?"

"Yep."

"Drum roll, please!"

Aunt Josie beat the tabletop with her hands and I opened my eyes slowly, wanting to prolong the surprise. What had she drawn, I wondered. It'd felt like they could be cartoon explosions. Or maybe bullet holes. It was really hard to tell. Whatever it was, though, it was going to be awesome.

"*Flowers?*"

"Cherry blossoms," she said. "How's that for a little bit of awesome?"

"Flowers."

"*Cherry blossoms* are badass."

"What? How?" I said. "On what *planet* could that even possibly—"

"On *this* planet! Just hear me out," said Aunt Josie. "The cherry blossom is a symbol of the samurai. And there's nobody out there more badass than they are."

She had a point.

"Because even though they were these fierce, brave warriors who could go totally berserkoid, they understood that like the cherry blossom, life was this beautifully fragile, precious thing that deserved the utmost respect. So riddle me this, Batman—what better symbol is there for a brave samurai warrior than a representation of the thing he held most dear?"

I looked at my new tattoo. Aunt Josie had drawn four blossoms—three were complete but a few petals of the fourth seemed to be floating away like they were on a breeze, and even though they had been drawn with Magic Markers, somehow Aunt Josie had made them appear delicate. I thought for a moment about how she'd said cherry blossoms were like life because they were so fragile. Then I thought about samurai warriors and how probably nobody ever teased them for liking flowers. They probably never got teased at all.

"You're right," I said. "Cherry blossoms *are* kinda badass."

"Toldja."

"They're the badassiest," I continued, figuring I should get the word out of my system while Mom wasn't around to hear it. "They're responsible for widespread badassery."

"Okay, settle down," she said. "Now what were you saying about the phone?"

"It's broken."

"No it's not."

"Yes it is," I said. "I've been calling and calling and nobody's answering at Budgie's house."

"Does it go to voice mail?"

"Yep."

"Have you left a message?"

"Fifteen."

"What?"

"Messages. I've left fifteen messages."

"First of all, you're a butt," she said, grabbing me and wrestling me into her lap. "And second, if it's going to voice mail it means *there's nobody home*!"

And that's when all the tickling started.

Budgie almost missed the bus on Monday morning. Phoebe's small, blue car pulled up just as it arrived. He didn't look like he wanted to talk about castles, though. He didn't look like he wanted to talk about anything. I wondered what happened but didn't ask. Budgie stomped to the back of the bus and I sat down next to this kid named Arlo who'd eat anything for a dollar.

"Guess what I have in my pocket," he said.

"No."

"A shrew," said Arlo. "I found it at the bus stop."

"A what?"

"A shrew. You know—like a tiny mouse."

"You found a shrew at the bus stop?"

"Yeah. I think it's dead."

"Why do you have a dead shrew in your pocket?"

"Because I found it."

"Yeah, but . . . never mind."

I looked down at my lap. I looked at the ceiling. I looked across the aisle out the window. I looked in every direction except Arlo's but it didn't matter because I could feel him staring at me.

"Got a dollar?"

"No."

When the bus got to school I jumped up and practically ran off but it wasn't because I couldn't wait to get inside and start learning. It was because I wanted to put as much space between me and Arlo as possible. I booked it down the hall and ended up being the first one in the classroom. That had never happened before. Even Ms. Dickson was shocked. Also I think I ruined Missy Sprout's day because she didn't get to be first this time. I wanted to tell her that this was a one-time thing for me and that I didn't like it any more than she did but she was glaring at me so bad that I actually got a little scared.

Budgie and Barely O'Donahue were the last two in from the playground. I tried to get Budgie's attention but couldn't because he was mostly staring at the floor. I heard him sit down and I started to turn around and then decided not to risk it. Missy Sprout was mad at me today and she just loved to tattle.

Recess finally came and on the playground Budgie, Barely O'Donahue, and a couple other kids were hanging out under the monkey bars. They had twigs in their mouths like they were cigarettes and were pretending to smoke because it was cold and you could see your breath.

"Hey, Budgie," I said. "Where were you yesterday?"

"What do *you* want?"

"I thought of some more cool stuff we could have in our castle."

Budgie kinda stopped. He quickly looked around at the other kids and then back at me.

"What castle?"

"You know—the one from Saturday. With the piranhadiles?"

"What's he talking about, Budgie?"

"Yeah, Budgie, what's he talking about? What castle?"

"I don't know," said Budgie. "Sounds pretty stupid."

"It's not stupid!"

"Yeah it is," said Budgie.

"You didn't think it was so stupid when we were at your house!"

"Dude, Lamb was at your house? I thought you said he was your archenemy."

"He is!"

"Did you guys have a playdate?"

"No, we didn't have a playdate!" said Budgie. "His mom couldn't get a babysitter or something. We were doing her a favor."

My eyes started to sting. I felt a knot rise in my throat. The other kids were laughing a little and Budgie just stood there looking proud of himself.

I didn't understand. We'd had so much fun Saturday afternoon that I thought we were friends again but now he was being meaner than ever and I hadn't even done anything.

"But we had fun!"

"I was just pretending," said Budgie. "And you believed it. Sucker! You're so lame!"

I just stood there. I couldn't think of what to say or what to do.

"Oh my God, are you *crying*?"

"No."

"Yes, you are! You're crying! Where's your cape, Captain Lame-ass?"

I suddenly wanted to grab Budgie's head in both hands. I wanted to squeeze it until my whole body shook. I wanted to squeeze until Barely O'Donahue and the other kids yelled for a teacher. I wanted to squeeze his fat head until it popped.

But when the end of recess bell rang, I stood there looking at Budgie without having said or done anything. My hands were shaking. My stomach felt like it was full of broken glass. The wind made the tears on my cheeks turn cold. Budgie and Barely O'Donahue and the rest went past me. Budgie even bumped me with his shoulder as he walked by.

"Loser."

I stood underneath the monkey bars until I was sure

Budgie and the others were gone. I stood there until I was the only one left on the playground and I would have stood there for the rest of my life if the recess monitor hadn't started yelling at me to come back to class.

I might have been the first one in the classroom this morning but I was the last one in after recess. I hung up my jacket and went to my desk and didn't say anything to anybody.

"You're late, Derek," said Ms. Dickson.

"Sorry."

"Please don't let it happen again," she said.

I stared at the top of my desk and didn't say anything, which must have been okay with Ms. Dickson because she started talking about something else. I was thinking about Budgie even though I didn't want to. In fact, I couldn't seem to stop thinking about him. Why would he say I was his archenemy? Had I done something to make him mad? I tried to remember everything we did on Saturday but thinking of all the fun we had just made me even more confused and angry.

"Ms. Dickson?"

"Yes, Derek."

"Can I go to the bathroom?"

"You may. But make it quick. You should have taken care of that during recess."

I didn't have to go during recess. I didn't even have to go now. I just couldn't sit in that room anymore. Not with Budgie there. I could feel him staring at the back of my head. I could hear the small whistle his nose made when he breathed. I even imagined I could smell eggs. But mostly I was frustrated and confused and sad and wouldn't be able to clear my head with Ms. Dickson trying to teach.

I felt better once I was in the hallway and even better once I was in the bathroom. I sat on the counter between the sinks, swinging my feet and turning the water on and off. No matter how hard I tried not to think about Budgie I thought about Budgie. I know Mom always said to be the bigger person but I just didn't want to anymore. Plus, I could eat a whale omelet for breakfast every day for the rest of my life and still not be a bigger person than Budgie.

I was thinking about stuff I could do to him for revenge but all my plans ended up needing things I just didn't have like an angry squirrel or a flamethrower. Then one of the stall doors opened and who should walk out but Arlo.

We looked at each other for a minute. At least I thought he was looking at me. His hair covered his eyes so it was kinda hard to tell exactly what he was looking at. He was pointed in my direction, anyway.

"What were you doing in there?"

"Sitting," he said. "What are you doing over there?"

"Also sitting."

"Cool."

Arlo blew some hair off his face. I wondered how many times he did that during the day and why he didn't just get a haircut or wear some kind of hat. At least now I knew he was looking at me and I suddenly realized that I might not have an angry squirrel or a flamethrower but I *was* standing about four feet away from something just as good.

I got back to the classroom and went right to my seat.

Arlo had driven a hard bargain for the shrew once I explained that I wanted to give him money *not* to eat it. He also wanted to shake hands and said we should spit on our palms first to make it more official because that was how men agreed on stuff in the old west. I wanted to tell him that we were neither men *nor* in the old west and that spitting in your hand was actually really gross but I didn't. Who was I to argue with a kid who, when all was said and done, would probably have eaten the shrew for free? I wasn't exactly sure what I was going to do with it just yet but I knew it was going to be epic. I mean, the shrew had it all—it was smelly, it was dead, it was small and would fit just about anywhere. Then I got an idea.

"Ms. Dickson?"

"Yes, Derek?"

"Can I go to the bathroom?"

"Weren't you just *in* the bathroom?"

"Yes. But I have to go again."

"Can't you wait until lunch?"

"No," I said. Then I added the only thing I could think of to make Ms. Dickson let me go the bathroom again.

"I'm having some, um . . . diarrhea."

The class exploded. Pretty much everybody started laughing and the girls who weren't laughing were making faces. Missy Sprout looked like she was going to faint.

"Do you need to go to the nurse?"

"I don't think so."

I got up and went to the door and opened it while Ms. Dickson tried to get the class to settle down. She told everyone that there was nothing funny about diarrhea, which only made everyone crack up again. I could still hear them laughing even after the door was closed.

I went to Budgie's cubby and got his lunch box. I took his lunch box into the bathroom and went into a stall and closed the door. I opened the lunch box and took out his sandwich and put the dead shrew inside of it. Then I put the sandwich back in the lunch box, closed the lid, and left the bathroom. After I'd put the lunch box back I returned to class and waited patiently for the lunch bell to ring.

Ms. Dickson talked about the presidents for a while and then she talked about European geography but the only two things I really heard were Millard Fillmore and Luxembourg and that was only because they sounded funny. Otherwise I was imagining Budgie biting into a peanut butter and shrew sandwich and screaming like a girl and how I'd be the hero of the school. I decided that, if it came to it, I wasn't above being carried around on everybody's shoulders.

The lunch bell finally rang. I'm not sure how it was possible but I'd swear it had taken four hours to get from ten thirty to twelve o'clock. Once we got to the cafeteria Budgie and Barely O'Donahue went and sat at a table with some of their friends from another class and right away Budgie leaned in and whispered something and then pointed at me.

I went past them and sat down at a table where I could see Budgie. I was worried that someone might sit with me and block my view but no one did. Budgie and Barely O'Donahue were now whispering to the kids who were sitting at nearby tables and some of them looked over at me and I could even hear a couple of them giggling. Then

Budgie put the palms of his hands against his mouth and blew a big raspberry and about half the cafeteria turned to look and started laughing.

"Now," I thought. "Everybody's looking! Open your lunch now!"

But he didn't. Instead, he stood up, got on his chair, and bowed, which made everyone laugh harder, and now some of them were starting to clap. Budgie was causing such a ruckus that a lunch monitor came over. She took Budgie's arm in one hand and his lunch box in the other and led him out of the cafeteria to eat his lunch alone in the classroom but I don't think he cared because he was waving and blowing kisses at everybody.

It wasn't fair. On any other day I bet he didn't even take the time to chew but today he didn't even open his lunch box. Now not only did I not get my revenge but also since the shrew thing didn't happen there was nothing to make everyone forget about the diarrhea thing so I was going to have to deal with being called "squirt" for the next week or so. The worst thing, though, happened in the middle of word study. I opened my desk to get a pencil sharpener and found the shrew right on top, which startled me so much I screamed.

I COULDN'T WAIT for the day to be over. All I wanted was to be at home and away from school but I had play rehearsal, which meant I'd have to stay even longer. Plus, Violet was going to be there and even though she was one of the only ones who didn't laugh or make fun of me or scream or pretend to faint or anything, she'd still been there and seen the whole thing and that was kind of embarrassing. Maybe if I didn't talk about it then neither would she.

She was sitting in a seat in the front row of the auditorium reading a book. I sat on the stage. Mr. Putnam had forgotten something and had gone to get it and it was uncomfortable sitting there with Violet in the empty auditorium and not saying anything. I decided to say something but when I opened my mouth I swear I thought different words were going to come out.

"I don't really have diarrhea."

Violet looked at me. I could feel my face turning red.

"Then why did you say you did?"

Budgie's face popped into my head. I didn't want it to but it did and now it was taking up all the room and I couldn't think about anything else. I felt myself getting angry so I jumped down from the stage and took off up the aisle.

"Where are you going?" Violet yelled after me.

I didn't answer her. Instead I went out into the hallway. It was quiet with all the kids gone and my footsteps seemed really loud as I paced back and forth. I wasn't really watching where I was going and I slipped on something and fell down. When I got up and looked around I found that I had stepped on a Magic Marker. I blamed Budgie. If he wasn't such a fat jerk none of this ever would have happened. I wished I'd never even met him. I picked up the Magic Marker and took the top off.

"What's a 'doosh'?" said Mr. Putnam behind me. "And who's Budgie?"

I blinked. The wall in front of me was covered in Magic Marker. Someone had written bad words about Budgie over and over again in big letters. There was something in my hand and I didn't have to look down to know what it was.

I wished I could just disappear. I closed my eyes tight and counted to ten but when I opened them I was still there. The words I'd written about Budgie were still on the

wall and the Magic Marker was still in my hand. I handed
it to Mr. Putnam.

"Do you know your way to the principal's office?" he
asked.

"Yes."

"Go there please. I'll be along in a minute."

"Mr. Putnam?"

"Yes."

"I'm sorry."

He just looked at me. Then he nodded and went into
the auditorium and I was alone in the hallway again. I
looked at what I'd written. It wasn't very nice. I'm not even
sure Budgie had been this mean. I licked my finger and
tried to rub off some of the Magic Marker but nothing happened. At the very least I was going to be back here with a
sponge and a bucket until the late bus came.

I gave the lady at the front desk my name and told her I
was there to see Mr. Howard. She picked up the phone and
pushed a button and said a few things and then hung up
and sort of nodded her head at the door.

Mr. Howard looked up from his desk when I came in.
His bald head was so shiny I swear I could see myself in it.
He also had a little beard that he was always petting like it
was a guinea pig or a hamster or something. There was a

candy jar on his desk, only instead of peanut butter cups or red hots it was full of paper clips. I wondered if that meant he kept candy in his paper clip dispenser and, if so, where he might be hiding it.

"Derek?"

"Yes sir?"

"Would you like to tell me why you're here?"

"No sir."

"Derek?"

"Yes sir?"

"Why are you here?"

"I wrote something."

"What was it?"

"Something bad."

"Where?"

"Um . . . the wall."

"Why?"

"I don't know," I said. "I think I was mad."

"You *think* you were mad?"

"Yes sir."

"Who were you mad at?"

"Budgie."

"And what did Budgie do?"

Mr. Howard put his elbows on his desk and looked at me and waited for me to answer. Budgie hadn't really done anything except hurt my feelings and that didn't seem like a good enough reason to write what I'd written.

"Nothing," I said. "He didn't really do anything."

"Then why did you write it?"

"I don't know," I said.

Mr. Howard stared at me. He petted his beard. After a minute he stood up and went to the door and opened it.

"Show me," he said.

On the way back to the auditorium we ran into Mr. Putnam. He stopped and we stopped and Mr. Putnam and Mr. Howard started talking. Unfortunately they were talking about me and what I'd done to the wall. Mr. Putnam even had the Magic Marker with him and he handed it to Mr. Howard, who looked at it and shook his head. I stood there wishing I could turn invisible like Fadeout or that I had Opaque's mutant ability to cloud people's minds. At this point I'd have even settled for Mysterion's lame Cloak of Obscurity. I didn't have any of those things, though, so mostly I just stared at my feet and felt bad.

The afternoon didn't get any better. In addition to scrubbing the wall clean, Mr. Howard said I'd have to stay after school every day for a *week* and scrub marker off all the walls, even in the girls' bathroom. Then he had me apologize to Mr. Putnam for wasting his time and Mr. Putnam said maybe the next time I decided to act like a hooligan I should first consider who might be affected by it. And if *that* wasn't enough, *then* Mr. Howard made me call home and tell *Mom* what happened, which was the worst part of all.

Mom was quiet on the phone. When she gets like that it means I've let her down and she's disappointed in me. I didn't like that. One time Budgie said that disappointing your parents was worse than making them mad because if your parents got disappointed too much they could stop loving you.

"I'm really sorry, Mom," I said.

"Me too."

"You still love me, though, right?"

I heard Mom clear her throat but she didn't say anything. There was just more quiet.

"Mom?"

"Of course I still love you, Derek. I'm just . . ." she took a deep breath and let it out.

"Disappointed?"

"Yes."

"But I said I was sorry."

"I know," she said. "Listen, I have to go now, Derek. Don't miss the late bus, okay?"

"Okay," I said. "And Mom? Mom?"

I was going to tell her that I loved her again so she

wouldn't forget but she wasn't there anymore. I really, *really* hoped Budgie was wrong.

Aunt Josie made a Mexican stew for dinner that had red chiles and pork in it and I only knew that because that's what she'd told me when I asked what was wrong with the chicken. I didn't remember ever having pork before but by the way the smell punched me in the face I didn't think I'd like it too much. Or at all. During dinner I made sure to fill up on tortilla chips so I wouldn't be able to finish it. Aunt Josie looked at me like she knew what I was doing but didn't say anything.

"I'm full," I said. "Is there anything for dessert?"

"I thought you were full."

"Well, I'm a little bit full. I saved some room for dessert."

"There isn't any."

"Not even a Chocolate Ka-Blam?"

"No," said Aunt Josie. "But if you're still hungry you could finish your *carne adobada*."

"My what?"

"Your stew."

I looked at the stew and the stew looked back. It seemed angry.

"I'm full," I said. "Can I be excused?"

"Fine," she said. "But no TV."

"What? Why not?"

"Because of what happened at school today. Your mom asked me not to let you watch TV."

"For how long?"

"What do you mean?"

"You know—one hour, two hours . . ."

"Dude, I think you're in a little more trouble than you realize."

"But that was at school! I can't get in trouble twice for the same thing can I?"

Then I remembered what Mr. Putnam said about my actions affecting other people and I wondered if this was what he'd been talking about.

"I don't know, Derek. She's pretty mad."

"I thought she was disappointed!"

"She's mad *and* disappointed."

"She can't be both!"

"You need to talk with her about it, Derek," said Aunt Josie. "She just asked me not to let you watch TV."

"But that's not fair!"

"I don't know what to tell you. Writing on the wall was something you chose to do. Nobody was holding a gun to your head."

"Why would someone hold a gun to my head?"

"It's just a figure of speech," said Aunt Josie. "Listen, I'm just doing what your mom asked me to do."

I went up to my room and shut the door and flopped down on my bed so hard the springs creaked. I could feel the frown on my face. It was deep—like someone had carved it there.

After what seemed like a long time I got down off my bed and went to my desk. The drawing I'd done of Castle Budgerek was sitting right on top. I picked it up and studied all the little details—the flamejobs on all the bumper cars and the cool expression on Budgie's face as he caught mad air off the half-pipe. I'd even drawn scales on the piranhadiles, which hadn't been easy.

I remembered how long it had taken me to do and how impressed Mom had been and how happy it had made her. Then I thought about how she wasn't happy anymore and how she was angry and disappointed instead and it was my fault for making her feel that way.

Suddenly I was crushing the drawing in my hands, crumpling it into a ball and throwing it on the floor. I stomped on it over and over again, then dropped to my knees and ripped it into a million pieces and threw them into the air. The next thing I knew, Aunt Josie was holding me. There were pieces of the torn drawing in her hair that reminded me of snowflakes. I heard someone sobbing. It was me.

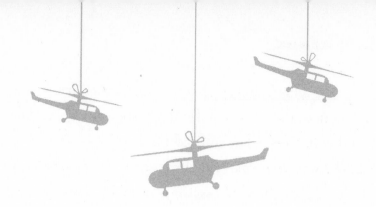

MY EYES OPENED in the morning before the alarm went off and I lay there looking up at the Apache helicopter. I took a deep breath and counted seventy-six Mississippis before letting it out. I wasn't looking forward to today. Not one bit.

Mom was in the kitchen when I got downstairs. She put frozen waffles in the toaster oven and we talked a little while waiting for it to ding. She didn't say anything about yesterday, though, and if she wasn't going to bring it up, then neither was I.

When the waffles were ready, Mom got the peanut butter and Marshmallow Fluff out of the cabinet and brought them to the table. Then she filled her mug with coffee and sat across from me, blowing on it a little before taking a sip.

"What happened yesterday?"

"What do you mean?"

"Derek."

"I got in trouble."

"I know that," she said. "What happened?"

I took a knife and spread peanut butter on one waffle and Fluff on the other and then pressed them together like a sandwich. I took a bite and chewed slowly. I didn't want to tell her it was all Budgie's fault because she was probably sick of hearing about him but I wasn't going to lie to her, either.

"Budgie called me a loser and said our castle was stupid," I said. I expected her to sigh or roll her eyes when she heard Budgie's name but she didn't. She looked troubled instead.

"I'm sorry, sweetheart. He shouldn't have said those things," she said. "You know your castle's not stupid, right?"

"I guess."

"What do you mean, you guess?"

I shrugged and stared at the waffle sandwich on my plate. I could feel Mom looking at me, waiting for me to say something.

"I guess it's not stupid."

"It's *not* stupid. It's the most creative thing I've ever seen," she said. "You two put a lot of thought into that castle and you should be proud. I know I am."

She smiled. I smiled, too. Then she frowned.

"But what I'm not proud of is what you did yesterday. Writing on the walls is called vandalism. People can go to jail for that."

"But Budgie—"

"But nothing," she said. "Look, Derek, I hate to say it but Budgie is going to keep on being Budgie. If you want to be his friend, then you need to figure out a way to not let him get to you."

"You mean be the bigger person, right?"

"I just mean you should find a way to live in the same world as Budgie that works for you—preferably one that doesn't land you in the principal's office."

Mom was still talking while I got my book bag and put on my sneakers but my mind was spinning so I wasn't really listening. Had she really said I didn't have to be the bigger person anymore?

"So you understand, right?" she said.

"Understand what?"

"That because of yesterday the TV is going to have to stay off for a while."

"What? For how long?"

"Two weeks."

"But what about the *Zeroman* special episode?"

"I'm sorry, Derek, but you should've thought of that before doing what you did."

"Nobody does that!" I blurted.

"Derek, stop. You're making it worse. Stop and think."

"No! It's not fair! It's Budgie's fault! It's *always* Budgie's fault!" I could feel myself getting angry. I couldn't stop.

"Then why isn't *he* the one staying after school for a week? Think about it."

"Stop telling me to think about it!"

Mom's mouth dropped open and her face went white. I don't think I'd ever yelled at her like that before. It was like I had slapped her. Then I noticed something else—the book I'd been putting in my backpack was no longer in my hand. It was lying on the counter where it had hit the drying rack with enough force to scatter silverware across the countertop and onto the floor. Mom stood up and went past me, her footsteps getting faster as she left the kitchen. They got even quicker as she went up the stairs and by the time I heard her bedroom door close she was practically running.

I didn't want anyone to sit next to me on the bus that morning. I didn't want to have to look at anyone or hear or smell them so it figured that as the bus filled up, who should sit next to me but Edwina Stubbs—the biggest, loudest, smelliest girl in school.

"Move in," she said.

I pulled my book bag onto my lap and moved over until

I was smashed up against the wall. Our arms were touching.

"I said move over!"

"I did!" I said. "There's no room left!"

She made a harrumphing sound that reminded me of farm animals, then she wiggled around in the seat and started talking real loud to someone who was at least two rows back. Somehow her book bag ended up in my lap, so not only was I totally squashed but now I was buried as well.

I tried to get comfortable but couldn't. It seemed like every time I moved—even a little—more of Edwina Stubbs would fill the space like she were a puddle. I closed my eyes and imagined her as a boneless, flesh-colored blob. In my mind, the Edwina puddle oozed down the fifth-grade hallway, absorbing the slower kids while the others ran screaming. By the time we got to school I imagined she'd absorbed the whole town and everyone in it.

"Hey! Quit trying to steal my bag!" she said, snatching it from my lap.

"But you're the one who put—"

"If anything is missing," she said, making a fist and holding it up to my face, "you'll get this. Got it?"

"We're gonna be late."

"Got it?"

"Just get off the bus."

"I'm watching you," Edwina said.

With that she oozed into the aisle with the other kids and stood in line waiting, tossing an occasional nasty look back my way. I sat with my book bag in my lap and planned to stay there until the driver kicked me off, suddenly feeling that being threatened by Edwina Stubbs was going to be the best thing that was going to happen to me today.

I wasn't wrong.

Ms. Dickson gave us a pop quiz I wasn't prepared for. At lunchtime I realized I'd forgotten to bring mine. Then at afternoon recess I got hit in the face with a kickball during a game I wasn't even in. The nurse said she hadn't seen a nose bleed like that in a long time like it was some big accomplishment but when I asked if I'd get an award or a plaque or something she just laughed.

That was Tuesday.

Wednesday wasn't much better.

And all I'm going to say about Thursday is that I was nowhere near Barely O'Donahue when the hamster bit him.

It didn't matter to me that Friday was rainy and cold. It didn't matter to me that Budgie took my hat on the bus, and the fact that I thought Montevideo was a movie rental place and not the capital of Uruguay only seemed to matter to Ms. Dickson. As far as I was concerned, all that mattered was that it was Friday and the school week was finally over.

When I got off the bus it wasn't really raining that hard anymore and by the time I got home it had stopped completely. Water filled the holes in the empty driveway. I let myself into the house and hung up my jacket and kicked off my shoes and dropped my book bag in the corner.

"Aunt Josie? Hello?"

I went to the pantry and got a Chocolate Ka-Blam. Then I went to the fridge and took out the milk and sat down at the table. I unwrapped the Ka-Blam, took a bite, and washed it down with a swig of milk from the jug. They tasted best that way. It was a scientific fact.

When I was done licking the last of the crumbs out of the wrapper and had taken a final gulp of milk, I put the cap back on the jug and put it back in the fridge. I saw the note when the door shut. It was stuck there with a magnet that looked like a baloney sandwich.

Derek—

Aunt Josie's car is finally fixed. I took her to pick it up. Be back soon. If you're going to have milk pls use a glass ok? And remember—no TV.
Love you—
Mom

I looked into the living room and could see part of the television. I looked out the kitchen window and could see part of the driveway. I wondered how soon "be back soon" was. I took a couple of steps toward the living room, stopped, and looked back. The driveway was still empty. I took a few more steps. Pretty soon I couldn't see the kitchen window anymore. Pretty soon after that I was sitting on the couch.

I stared at the television. I rubbed my hands on my pants and swallowed. My heart was beating so fast I thought it would explode out of my chest. I squinted my ears and listened for Mom's car in the driveway or the banging of the storm door but didn't hear either of them.

I picked up the remote and pointed it at the television. Was I really going to do this? My thumb hovered over the red power button for a second or two like I was giving someone or something a last chance to stop me. I listened for Mom's car again and didn't hear it. I closed my eyes and slowly pressed the button.

Mom must have been watching the news before because when I opened my eyes I wasn't looking at *Zeroman* or *A Dog Named Cat* or even *Jenny Rainbow and the Starlight Pony Squad*. Instead I was looking at two people behind a desk and a lot of numbers and little symbols moving across the bottom of the screen. The volume was also turned way down. I flipped to a cartoon channel but Mom had blocked it. I flipped to another cartoon channel but she'd blocked that one also. I tried all the channels I could think of that might be showing something I'd want to watch but I was locked out of all of them. She'd even blocked the Adventure Kids channel and that one was educational.

I slumped back into the couch and sat there staring at the screen. Fine. I might not have been able to watch TV but if Mom thought that would get me to do homework instead, she was crazy. I switched back over to the news channel. The last thing I needed was for her to turn on the TV and have it be on one of the channels she'd blocked. I'd learned that one the hard way.

I wasn't sure it was the same channel Mom had been watching because all those news people look the same to me. The same numbers and little symbols moved across the bottom of the screen. The only thing different from before was that there was a picture of a soldier in the corner.

He was wearing desert camo and looking at the camera with a serious expression on his face. I bet he had a code name. I bet it was Sandstorm or something cool and desert related like that. The soldier looked kinda familiar, too, but I couldn't place him.

Then I pictured him without his helmet on and instead of jeeps in the background I imagined our backyard and the way it looked when he held me by the wrists and swung me around until my feet came off the ground and I couldn't hear anything but the roar of the wind and the sound of my own laughter.

"Mom! Mom! Come quick," I shouted, jumping up and banging both knees on the table. The remote fell from my hand and struck the table in such a way that the batteries came flying out. "Dad's on TV! I think he won the war!"

I was so excited to see my father I'd forgotten I was the only one in the house but I didn't have time to feel embarrassed. I didn't have time to put the batteries back in the remote either so I scrambled over the table and launched myself at the television, flipping open the control panel and searching like crazy for the volume button.

The news people were talking about my dad and I was missing it. I tried to read their lips while I stabbed blindly for the volume button with my finger. I was pretty sure they'd just said my dad had not only won the war all by himself but he had also saved the president and they couldn't say it on TV if it wasn't true.

I could feel my smile bumping up against the boundaries of my face, pushing against them, threatening to break through. Maybe Dad could come home now. Maybe it could be for good this time. I found the volume button, pressed it, and held it down. It was easier to read lips with the sound turned up. They weren't talking about the president after all.

When my mom came home I was still sitting there. A minute could have passed. Or a day. Or a week. At some point she must have pulled into the driveway but I hadn't heard it. The storm door must have banged when she'd come inside but I hadn't heard that either. I almost hadn't heard her put the groceries down or call my name—once in anger when she saw I was watching TV and another time in sadness when she saw what I was watching. She came to me quickly and scooped me into her lap, putting herself between me and the television.

"Oh no," she said. "Oh no. Oh no. Oh no."

And she kept saying it, too, until the words just came together and weren't really words anymore. I don't think she even stopped to breathe. My face was pressed into her neck and when I lifted up my head I was looking at the world through the auburn curtain of her hair. On TV a girl in a raincoat with an umbrella and a microphone was standing in front of our house looking wet and serious.

"Mom?"

"Yes, baby?"

"Our house is on TV."

"I know."

"Why is our house on TV?"

"Because they're vultures!" spat Aunt Josie, storming into the room and stabbing the television off with her finger. The telephone rang and Aunt Josie stomped off to get it. I overheard her say a few words I probably shouldn't have. Mom was sobbing now and it was hard to tell who was holding who anymore.

I could see myself reflected in the blank TV screen—my small, white face peeking over my mom's shoulder and my hands clasped around her neck. Even in the reflection you could tell she was shaking.

Words floated in my head—words the news people had said—words I knew the meaning of but wished I didn't. Words like "missing" and "body." There were others, too, like "rocket."

And "dead."

I let go of Mom and stood up and found the batteries and put them back in the remote. Then I sat on the couch, pointed it at the television, and pressed the power button. The news came back on. My dad's picture was back in the corner. The news people were talking about him.

"Derek, don't," Mom said. Her voice was tiny and weak and for some reason I thought of baby birds, alone and blind and helpless. "I don't want you to hear—"

"I want to watch cartoons."

Mom was still kneeling on the floor in front of the television. Her shoulders were slumped and her head was down.

"Derek, I—"

"Cartoons."

She straightened up a little and turned, pulling her hair out of her face with her fingers and putting it behind her ears. Her cheeks were wet and her bottom lip was bleeding. She must have bitten it. Some hair fell back in her face but this time she didn't move it.

"I meant to—I didn't know how—"

"*Cartoons!*" I exploded, screaming so loud I hurt my neck. "*Cartoons, cartoons, cartoons!*"

Mom jumped and in the kitchen Josie dropped something. It broke. I could tell by the sound. Mom took the remote from me and entered the code to unlock the kid channels. I sat on the couch with my arms folded and my chin all down into my chest like I was a turtle hiding in its shell.

The Adventure Kids channel was on and some kid in one of those safari helmets was letting a big tarantula walk up his arm. It was orange and black and moved slowly, its two front legs feeling the air. The kid was saying how its legs were covered in these tiny hairs and how they itched and tickled him at the same time.

Mom still knelt in front of the television and the way she was kneeling made me think of a marionette with the strings cut. If you put a lamp on her head she'd be a table. I laughed at that. I couldn't help it. On TV the tarantula was now on the kid's face. I laughed at that, too. I probably would have kept on laughing forever if I hadn't suddenly thrown up all over the table.

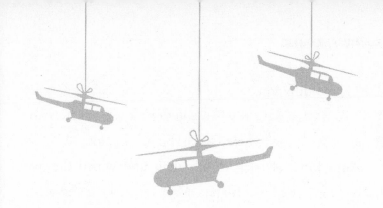

WE DIDN'T EAT DINNER that night. Nobody thought to make it and I didn't think any of us were hungry anyway. Mom went from kneeling in the living room to sitting in the kitchen. The phone rang a lot and after a while Aunt Josie stopped answering it. I think she may have gotten tired of me asking her who it was.

"It's people who heard about your dad calling to say how sorry they are," she said.

"Why are they sorry?" I asked. "They didn't do it."

"It's called sympathy, Derek," she said. "They feel bad for us because we lost your dad."

"But we didn't lose Dad," I said.

"Oh, Derek." Aunt Josie blinked a few times fast. If she was trying to hold back tears it didn't work. "You do know he's . . . gone. You understand what that means, right?"

"Yeah, but he's not lost."

"Derek, sweetheart, yes he is."

"No, he's not. He *was* lost," I said. "But then they found him. He was in a cave."

"That's different."

"No it's not. Lost is when you don't know where something is. We know where Dad is. So he's not lost."

Aunt Josie sat back in her chair and wiped the tears from her eyes with her fingers. Mom cleared her throat and spoke. Her voice was soft but even.

"Isn't your show on now, Piggy?"

"What show?"

"With the special episode? *Zeroguy*?"

"You mean *Zeroman*?"

"That's it."

"Aren't I still punished?"

"You've been punished enough."

Her face was pale in the kitchen light. Except for her eyes, which were red with dark circles underneath. She started to smile but stopped. Maybe she realized it was stupid to smile and pretend everything was okay when we both knew it wasn't.

"Why don't you go to the living room and watch your show, okay?"

"Can I just go to my room instead?"

"Of course you can but I thought—I mean, you've waited so long to watch your show."

"I know. It'll be on again though."

I didn't want to look at my mom so I looked at my hands instead. They were sort of dirty. My pen had leaked at school today and there was a big blue ink smudge on my finger, and out of my ten fingernails, six needed cutting.

"Don't bite your nails," Mom said, "you'll get worms in your belly."

I put my hand back in my lap, not liking the way Mom was looking at me. It seemed like she was studying me, trying to guess what I might do or say next. I was used to people at school looking at me like that but I didn't expect it from her. I always thought she knew me better.

"Sorry."

"You don't have to be sorry."

"Can I go to my room, please? I really just want to go to my room right now."

"Would you like me to come with you?"

I heard her but didn't answer. Instead, I stood up and left the kitchen and when I heard her say she loved me I didn't respond to that either. The phone rang again as I climbed the stairs to my room and the last thing I heard before closing my door was Mom's tortured cry and the sound of the phone being torn from the wall.

Dear Derek—

How's my guy?

I'm writing this in my bed in the field hospital. Don't worry though I'm fine. Your daddy just did kind of a dumb thing. I woke up the other day with a bellyache and I didn't tell anybody right away and it got worse and worse until I couldn't even walk. The doctor said I had a bad infection in my belly called peritonitis and they had to do an operation to fix it.

Now I have to wait until I'm better before I can fly again and guess what—it's called being "grounded." Funny, huh? I didn't think grown ups could get grounded, did you? Anyway I hope getting better doesn't take long. The longer I'm here the more missions I'll be passed over for and I don't like not doing my part.

I hope school is going well and that we'll see each other soon!

Much love,

Dad

The Knight Rider lunch box was on the floor—on its side and empty. I'd taken all of the envelopes out of it and all of the letters out of the envelopes and my bed was now a sea of paper. I was adrift in the middle of it, clinging to the last one hundred and fifty-five words my father had written me—hanging on to the letter as if it were a life raft. He'd used six hundred and thirty-three letters and had written seven paragraphs including the salutation and whatever the part where you put "sincerely" was called.

When I finished reading the letter I read it again. Apart from comic books, the letters from my dad were the only things I read more than once. I usually read them two or three times each time I sat down with them. I had even memorized whole parts of them completely by accident.

I lay back on my bed and closed my eyes, the letters crinkling loudly underneath me. Then I rolled over and faced the wall because I didn't want to see the helicopter model when I opened them. I saw it anyway. In my head. Only it wasn't the model, it was the real thing and it was getting hit with a rocket over and over again and spinning to the ground and crashing.

I didn't want to think about my dad but I couldn't help it. In my head he is struggling with his safety harness. His hands are shaking. I imagine the strong smell of gasoline from a busted fuel line. He calls out to the gunner but the gunner doesn't answer because the gunner is dead. Black smoke starts to fill the cockpit. It is thick and oily and it smells bad because the gunner's body is starting to burn.

I shook my head and shut my eyes and tried to think about something else. I tried to put all fifty states in alphabetical order but I'd only gotten as far as Delaware before I was imagining my dad dragging himself across some sharp rocks to get away from a burning helicopter. His legs are bent funny. His hands are covered in dirt and blood.

Florida, Georgia, Hawaii, Idaho . . .

The sun is going down and the sky is red. Dad is pulling himself toward a split in the rocks. I imagine his flight suit has been torn away at the elbows and the flesh underneath is like raw hamburger.

. . . Illinois, Indiana, Iowa . . .

The cave is small. Light from the last bit of sunset has found its way inside but it will be gone soon. My dad has drawn his sidearm and is sitting with his back against the cold rocks facing the entrance. His face is covered in sweat. He is sitting in a puddle of blood. The puddle is spreading quickly.

. . . Kansas, Kentucky, Louisiana . . .

His sidearm becomes heavy and he puts it down. After a while he closes his eyes.

. . . Maine . . .

A little while after that he stops bleeding.

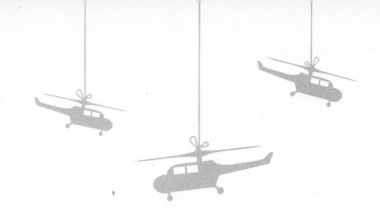

I DIDN'T REMEMBER falling asleep but I must have because the next thing I knew it was morning. I tried to roll over but I couldn't. Somebody was in bed with me and their arm was around my waist, pinning me down.

I tried to wiggle out and heard a crinkling, crackling sound and that was when I remembered there were letters all over the bed. That was also when I remembered about my dad.

I stopped wiggling then. I just lay there on my side facing the wall. The arm around my waist felt heavy. I had a feeling it was Mom's because on cold mornings when I was little I'd get into bed with Mom and Dad and she'd hold me like this under the covers and I'd feel warm and safe. I didn't feel very safe this time though. I felt whatever the exact opposite was.

I breathed. I blinked. I stared at the wall. After a while I smelled coffee. Mom woke up and moved her arm leaving a cold spot on my side. She shifted. The letters crackled. I didn't move.

"Derek?"

I didn't want to talk. I pretended to sleep.

"I know you're not asleep."

"How'd you know?"

"I didn't but now I do."

"You tricked me?"

"A little."

"You shouldn't be tricking me at all," I said. "I'm just a kid."

"I know. You're right. I'm sorry."

I wished I wasn't against the wall because I wanted to get up and leave. I couldn't though, because Mom's arm was across me again and I just knew she wasn't about to let me move it. She meant to have a Talk. And when Mom meant to have a Talk there wasn't much you could do about it even if you weren't pinned to the bed.

"How are you feeling?" she asked.

We lay there for a little while and didn't say anything. I thought maybe she'd fallen asleep again.

"Derek?"

"I'm not sure," I said.

"What do you mean?"

I scratched my arm and thought for a second. What *did* I mean?

"I dunno," I said finally. "I feel kinda . . . empty. Is it okay to feel empty?"

"Any way you feel is how you feel and that's okay. Especially now," Mom said. "And when those feelings change, the new ones will be okay, too. People will understand if you're sad or if you're angry—"

"But I'm not sad or angry. I told you, I'm not feeling anything. Just empty. And my head hurts. That's how I'm feeling."

She moved her arm from around my waist and started stroking my hair with her hand. I pictured her with a worried look on her face, her lips pressed together so you couldn't see them.

"Is there something you want to talk about?" she asked.

"Like what?"

"Anything."

"No thanks."

I listened to her breathe for a minute or two. Her breath was a little bit choppy and I was pretty sure she was crying. Or trying not to. She kept on stroking my hair.

"Would you like a song?"

I hadn't had a song in a long time. Dad usually sung them to me.

"Yeah."

"What song do you want?" she asked, clearing her throat a little.

"'Sunday Morning Coming Down.'"

"What? How do you know that song?"

"Dad sings it to me."

"He does?"

"Yeah. It's Johnny Cash."

"I know who it is. I'm just not sure you're old enough to—why don't we do 'Ring of Fire' instead?"

"What about 'Boy Named Sue'?"

"'Boy Named—'?" She laughed. I think it surprised her. "Is there anything your father won't sing to you?"

"Yeah," I said. "The Jonas Brothers."

We finally agreed on "Walk the Line" and she cleared her throat again and started to sing. She didn't really know all the words, though, so she sang the ones she did know and la-la-la'd the rest. I was warm with her body pressed against mine. Her fingers were in my hair.

"How many days did they search before they found Dad?" I said.

Mom stopped singing.

"What?"

"Those people on the news said they found Dad after days of searching. How many days was it?"

"I don't know," she said.

"Was it four days?"

"I—I don't know."

"A week?"

"Stop it."

"Ten days?"

"Derek, stop. It wasn't ten days," Mom said. "It was . . . it was nine. Nine days."

"Oh."

Suddenly I didn't feel so warm anymore. It was like the whole room had gotten colder even though I knew it hadn't. I curled into a ball and hugged my knees but it didn't help. At that moment I didn't think anything would.

"How do you know?"

"There was a man—a soldier—an . . . officer. He came to the house last week while you were at school," Mom said. She was playing with my hair, twirling it around one of her fingers. I didn't think she knew she was even doing it.

"What day?"

"Thursday."

"I had rehearsal that day with Violet and Mr. Putnam."

"Okay."

"We went over the blocking for our scene."

"Okay."

"Blocking is how the actors know where to go onstage."

"Okay," Mom said. "Is there anything else?"

"Violet doesn't have a television."

"Derek."

"Isn't that weird?"

"Derek, don't you want to hear my story?"

"Not really."

"Why not?"

"Because I already know how it ends."

I reached out and placed my palm flat against the wall, feeling the plaster that was a little bit rough in some places and a little bit smooth in others. It was cold. I could hear Aunt Josie moving around downstairs. I held my palm against the wall for as long as I could, until it got too cold, then I put it between my legs to warm it.

"I'm going to tell the story anyway," Mom said. "For me. You don't have to listen."

I held my palm against the wall again. Longer this time. Till I was sure my fingers would snap off. I pictured them breaking like twigs, coming off neatly at the knuckle and falling between my bed and the wall. I imagined them being carried away by mice.

"An officer came to the house last week," Mom started again. "His name was Llewellyn Moore. He was a captain. He told me that your father's helicopter had been shot down in Afghanistan and he was missing and that they were looking for him and he was sorry.

"After he left I stood there. In the doorway. Just staring down the driveway for I don't know how long. At first I told myself it was all a mistake and that I was standing there because I knew he'd come back and apologize but deep down I knew it was because if I let go of the doorknob I'd fall down."

Mom kept talking, telling me the story of the worst week of her life—how she panicked every time the phone rang, how she stopped eating and couldn't sleep without having nightmares. She told me that one day she even tore the house apart looking for hidden cameras because she'd become convinced that she was on a reality TV prank show and that Aunt Josie had come home and found her sitting on the kitchen floor crying in the middle of a pile of broken dishes.

"But Aunt Josie said she—"

"I know she did," said Mom. "She was covering for me."

"Why didn't you tell me?"

"I didn't want you to worry," Mom said. "I've never felt so helpless and scared. It crushed me. It almost killed me. Not knowing if your father was alive or dead made me sick. I just couldn't do that to you."

"Oh."

"Then yesterday morning Captain Moore came back and well . . . now I know. I was going to tell you. I swear I was. I never, ever meant for you to find out that way."

I didn't say anything. It was kinda hard to breathe. My chest suddenly felt like someone was sitting on it.

"He's actually a very nice man."

"Do you think he was scared?"

"I don't know about scared—a little nervous maybe. It must be hard to give such bad news to a complete stranger."

"I'm not talking about *that* guy. I don't care about him," I said. "I'm talking about Dad."

"Oh."

"Do you think Dad was scared? Y'know—in the end?"

It was Mom's turn to not say anything. Maybe she hadn't thought about that. I thought about that kind of thing all the time.

"I don't think he was scared," I said. "I bet he was brave."

"Fear is natural, Derek. There's nothing wrong with being afraid."

"Budgie says only wussies say stuff like that."

"Budgie's an idiot," Mom said. "Would you like to know what true bravery is? True bravery is all about *conquering* fear; so in order to be brave you have to be afraid first. You can't have one without the other."

I thought about that for a minute. Then I remembered a couple of things Budgie had done that I thought were brave but now I wasn't so sure.

"What about the time Budgie made those wings and jumped off his garage?" I asked.

"That wasn't brave. That was stupid," Mom said. "But getting back to your father, I *do* think he was scared but only because he was in a scary situation. I do *not* think, however, that he would let fear stop him from doing what he needed to do."

What she said about bravery made sense. What she'd said about Budgie had also made sense. He *was* kind of an idiot. Now that I thought about it, making wings out of two old umbrellas and jumping off a garage had never seemed stupider.

I thought for a little while about fear and courage. I thought about my dad and wondered what it must have been like toward the end. Had he known he was dying? Did his life flash before his eyes? Was he thinking of me and Mom? Of home?

In the movies the dying soldier always pulls out a picture of his family and traces the surface of it with a trembling, bloody finger. Then, right before he dies, he says something like, "I'm sorry we never got to build that tree house, Billy," and the picture slips from his hand and the camera follows it to the ground.

I didn't know if Dad even *had* a picture of me with him. If he did, I hoped it wasn't the goofy one from first grade where my hair's all messed up and I'm missing my two front teeth. That would be embarrassing.

"Does your life really flash before your eyes right before you die?"

"That's what they say."

"All of it or just parts?"

"I don't know."

"And does it happen with all types of death or just the ones where you have time to think?"

"What do you mean?"

"Because if it happened suddenly like in a car crash and only *parts* of your life flashed before your eyes and they all happened to be the bad parts, then well . . . don't you think that'd be kind of a rip-off?"

"I suppose that would be a rip-off. That's why I think probably only the good parts flash by. Like a highlight reel."

"What's a highlight reel?"

"It's like a movie of only the best parts."

"Hm."

"Indeed."

"So what's on your highlight reel?"

"Let's see—my highlight reel," said Mom, sniffling a little. "The day I met your dad, obviously. Our wedding day. God, we were so young."

"What else is on it?"

"The day you were born and every day since."

We were quiet for a little while then.

"Do you think I was on Dad's highlight reel?"

"Derek, I think you *were* Dad's highlight reel. He was so proud of you. It was like you were all he ever talked about."

"Really?"

"Yes," said Mom. "And frankly I got sick of hearing it after a while."

"Really?"

"Of course I didn't get sick of it. Turkey."

"But he *did* talk about me?"

"Yes."

"A lot?"

"All the time."

It felt good to know my dad had spoken of me because it meant he'd been thinking about me as well and it was nice to be thought of. And if he'd been thinking about me in the end, then he hadn't really died alone after all. Not really.

"Mom?"

"Yes?"

"Why did he go have to go back?" I asked. "I thought he was finished."

"He was."

"Then why did he go back?"

"Because when he enlisted he signed a piece of paper saying he would if they needed him," said Mom. "And I guess they did. I know it doesn't seem fair."

"That's because it's *not* fair. So he signed a piece of paper—so what? It's not like he took a blood oath or anything. Wait, he didn't, did he?"

"No, he didn't," said Mom. "But he gave them his word."

"So?"

"So sometimes in this life your word is all you have," said Mom, "and if you are an honorable person—a person with strong character—you will stick by your word even if you don't want to."

"And did Dad?"

"Did Dad what?"

"Want to?"

"No of course not," said Mom. "But he did. And I know for a fact it was the hardest thing he ever had to do."

"How?"

"Because having to say good-bye to your father again was the hardest thing *I* ever had to do."

The phone rang and I heard Aunt Josie answer it. Then I heard her coming up the stairs and down the hall. My bedroom door was open so she knocked a little on the frame.

"You guys awake up here?" she asked. "Annie? It's for you."

"I'm with Derek right now, Jo. Can I call them back?"

"I think you'll want to take this. It's the army."

Mom rolled over and got out of bed, taking the phone from Aunt Josie and stepping into the hallway. Josie stood there like she didn't know what to do—like she was wondering if she should stay in here with me or go join her sister. In the end she stayed standing right where she was and offered me a sad kind of smile. I did my best to smile back. I'm not sure it worked.

Mom came back in and sat down on the bed, the letters crackling underneath her. She took my hand. Held it. I didn't let go because I figured that, at that moment, she needed somebody to hang on to. Aunt Josie sat on Mom's other side and took her other hand. We stayed like that for a while. Connected. Just being there.

Mom started to say something but she stopped and cleared her throat a little. Then she tried again.

"Jason's coming home," she said.

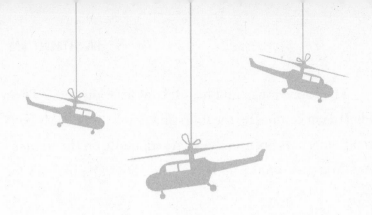

MR. HOWARD MET ME when I got off the bus on Monday morning. It was cold and windy and his bald head was chapped. I wondered how long he'd been standing there. He was wearing big wool mittens and a matching scarf and it didn't look like his little beard was doing a good job of keeping his face warm because the tip of his nose was red and drippy.

"Good morning, Mr. Lamb," he said. "How are you feeling today?"

The wind yanked the breath from his mouth and carried it off.

"Okay I guess. A little tired."

Kids moved quickly around Mr. Howard and me as we walked to the door, and I caught a couple of them looking back over their shoulders at me. They must have thought I was public enemy number one to have the principal meet me at the bus like that. I wondered what they thought I'd done. I hoped they thought it was something cool.

"Could I speak with you for a moment in my office?"

"I don't want to be late."

"I'm the principal, Derek. It's okay," he said. "I'll give you a note for you to give to Ms. Dickson when we're done."

Mr. Howard put his hand on my shoulder and steered me into his office. He closed the door and pulled his mittens off and started to unwind his scarf. It was longer than I thought it'd been. It just kept going and going. When he was finished he sat down and opened a binder on his desk and looked at a page. Then he pushed it away and leaned forward and put his elbows on his desk. He cleared his throat before speaking.

"Derek, I—that is to say—we here at the school—the administration and the faculty have—" he said, pulling the binder to him and checking the page again. When he looked up it was right into my eyes.

"We were all so very sorry to hear about your father, Derek, and I wanted to let you know that if you needed to talk or—or anything—that we're here to listen. My door is always open."

"Okay."

I think Mr. Howard expected me to say more things but I didn't so we just looked at each other instead—almost like a staring contest. We stayed like that for a while.

"Can I ask you something?" I said.

"Of course."

"It's something I've been wondering about."

"Of course. Go ahead."

"Why do you keep paper clips in your candy jar?"

"I'm sorry?"

"It says 'candy' right on it but there's no candy," I said. "That seems a little bit like cheating."

"It used to have candy in it," Mr. Howard said. "But I noticed the same few students were turning up here more and more often—twice, sometime three times a week, and I suspected it was because of the candy. So when I ran out I filled it with paper clips and I haven't seen them since."

I didn't have any more questions and there wasn't anything I felt like talking about. Mr. Howard told me again how his door was always open if I needed anything. Then he wrote a note to Ms. Dickson and handed it to me.

"Wait, Derek, there's one more thing."

He got something out of the top drawer and put it down on the desk.

"A peanut butter cup?" I said. "I thought you said you didn't have any candy in here."

"All I said was I didn't keep candy in the jar. I never said anything about not having any candy in the office." He winked. "Have a good day, Mr. Lamb."

When I got back to the classroom everybody was doing math. On the whiteboard was another word problem about Kate and Timmy. This time Timmy had taken one-third of Kate's apples. He was always doing stuff like that and it made me wonder why Kate was friends with him at all.

I went in and put Mr. Howard's note on Ms. Dickson's desk and took my seat. When I looked up I noticed some kids staring at me. This one kid in the front row named Xavier had even turned all the way around.

"I should be seeing eyes, not backs of heads," said Ms. Dickson.

Xavier and the other kids faced front again and Ms. Dickson went back to the problem on the board. I was glad she'd said something but I didn't have to turn around to know some of the kids behind me were still staring. I scrunched down into my chair and tried to become invisible. I guess it kinda worked because normally when I do that Ms. Dickson tells me to stop slouching and sit up straight but this morning she didn't. She didn't even call on me for answers or anything. I mean, she barely even looked in my direction. Then after recess she asked us to open our desks and take out our history workbooks and that's when I found the envelope. It was cream colored and had my name written on it.

I looked around to see if anyone else had gotten one but

they were all pretty much fumbling around in their desks or trying to find the right page in the book or whatever so I figured it was just me. Then I looked up at Ms. Dickson and, for the first time today, she was looking right back at me. She smiled. Then the corners of her mouth turned down a little and she put her hand over her heart. It seemed strange but in that moment it was like she stopped being my teacher and became my friend instead. I slid the card out of the envelope.

> *Derek,*
> *There are far too many Rory McReadys*
> *in the world and not enough Jason Lambs.*
> *With my deepest sympathies,*
> *Charlotte Dickson*

I wondered who Rory McReady was for a second and then I remembered. He had been in my dad's eighth-grade English class and was the one who kept throwing his desk at Ms. Dickson. I felt myself smile a little. Not because of the desk-throwing thing but because I totally understood what she meant. I wanted to send her some kind of signal but when I looked up from the card the moment was over and she was a teacher again.

The rest of the day went like the morning had—kids looking at me when they thought I couldn't see them but I could. I could see them. It made me feel uncomfortable and I didn't like it. When we were let out at the end of the day I was surprised to see Mr. Howard waiting in the hall outside the classroom. He took me aside as the rest of the kids passed us on their way to the buses. I noticed a few kids looking over at me. I heard my name whispered. It was starting to make me angry.

"What are you looking at?"

"Come on, Derek, that's not necessary."

"They've been staring at me all day and I'm sick of it."

"They're uncomfortable. They don't know how to act or what to say around you."

"They did last week."

"Last week was different."

"But I'm still the same person."

"I know you are, Derek. And Ms. Dickson and the rest of the teachers and a lot of your classmates know you are, too. It's just that some people—the ones who are doing the staring—do not. Not everybody deals with this sort of thing the same way and you have to allow them time to come to terms with it."

"No I don't," I muttered.

"What?"

"I don't have to allow them to do anything. It's none of their business," I said. "It's not even any of *your* business."

He stopped walking but I didn't. I walked faster.

Then I started to run.

Play rehearsal went fine and afterward we all sat on the edge of the stage while Mr. Putnam gave notes to everybody. He said me and Violet's scene was good but that I had to remember to let her lead me offstage when we exited. He also said I needed to project more and I nodded even though I didn't really know what he was talking about.

Then he reminded us that since we opened this Thursday, tomorrow and Wednesday's rehearsals would be full run-throughs in costume, but I wasn't worried. I was actually getting excited. Mom was going to be there and probably Aunt Josie was, too. I pictured them standing up and cheering for me the second the lights came up and they saw me onstage and I imagined the rest of the audience joining them.

"I've recruited some students to assist you backstage with props and costumes and so forth," Mr. Putnam was saying. "They'll be new at this so please treat them with respect. Violet, Derek—two of them are girls from your class, I believe."

"Really?" said Violet. "Who?"

"Let's see, Ms. Dickson's class . . ." Mr. Putnam picked up a piece of paper and looked at it over the top of his glasses. "Ah, here we go. Helping us from Ms. Dickson's class will be Melissa Sprout and Marion—"

Mr. Putnam sneezed suddenly and everyone jumped. Violet even screamed a little. He pulled a handkerchief from the pocket of his coat and blew his nose into it, making a sound like a trumpet. His cheeks had gone red.

"Mr. Putnam," I said. "There's no Marion in our class."

"Then who is Marion Pratt?"

My heart sank, pushing whatever good mood I had right out through my toes. I remembered now, there *was* a Marion in our class. It just wasn't a girl.

"It's Budgie, sir."

It had been the very first secret shared at the very first meeting of the original Secret Secret Club and I'd been keeping it for so long I'd completely forgotten about it until now, and now that I was thinking about it I remembered that was also the day he told me how he'd gotten his nickname. I'd asked him and since we were in the Fort of Truth he had to answer. It was one of the rules.

"A budgerigar. A budgie bird," he'd said. "Y'know, a parakeet?"

Then he told me that when he was little he was always copying the sound of people's voices and his grandmother thought it was adorable because it reminded her of a pet parakeet she used to have that did the same thing until one day it got out of its cage and the cat ate it.

"So one time at dinner, she said, 'Budgie, could you pass the rolls.'"

"That doesn't seem so bad."

"Yeah, well," said Budgie, "it was during Thanksgiving dinner. So the whole family was there."

"Oh," I said. "What was the bird's name?"

"Sissy."

I remember wanting to laugh really, really badly but not wanting to open my mouth until I was sure I wouldn't.

"Well," I'd said carefully. "I'd say you got lucky."

"Thank you, Mr. Lamb," said Mr. Putnam, making a note on the paper. Then Violet said that since names were being corrected, Melissa Sprout would probably like to be called Missy instead, so Mr. Putnam made a note of that as well.

"Mr. Putnam?" I asked. "Where did that list come from?"

"The attendance office."

"The attendance office?"

"Yes," Mr. Putnam said. "Why? Are you wearing a wire?"

"What? No. I'm just—it's just that his mother is the only one who calls him Marion."

"Then she must have been the one to fill out all the paperwork at the beginning of the school year," Mr. Putnam said. "Okay if I continue here?"

I nodded slowly, a feeling of impending doom beginning to seep in around the edges of me. It was bad enough that I'd broken the Secret Secret Club's only rule by sharing a secret with nonmembers and now I may have made it worse by talking about it. I needed to give them something else to think about instead.

"I was born with a tail," I blurted.

I didn't know if that was going to be enough for them to forget the Marion thing but I had to be sure. Me and Budgie might not have been friends anymore but a club was a club and what was said there was supposed to stay there.

"And my middle name is Dorothy."

I had trouble falling asleep that night even though I was tired. Someone had taken down the Apache helicopter. It was probably my mom but I just didn't have the energy to ask her about it. I tried looking at a different model. I looked at the F-14 Tomcat. I looked at the Spitfire. I even looked at the B-52 Stratofortress but it wasn't the same. I couldn't imagine myself flying any of them the way I could the Apache. I couldn't imagine my dad at all. It was like I'd forgotten him.

I rolled onto my side and looked out the window. The moon was cold. The yard shivered. I pulled the quilts up around my neck and closed my eyes. Everything I did in my dreams that night I did alone.

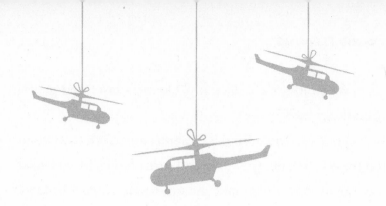

"HI, PIGGY. HOW'D YOU sleep?" Mom said without looking up from the bowl of batter.

"Are we having pancakes?"

"How'd you know?"

"You're using the green bowl," I said. "You always use the green bowl to make pancakes."

"I do?"

"Yeah."

The ingredients were spread out over the counter. The flour canister was open. The milk was still out. So was the butter tub. There were eggshells in the measuring cup. I went to the fridge and got the orange juice out and poured a glass and sat at the table and watched her stir the pancake batter. I couldn't remember the last time she'd made pancakes from scratch. She usually got the just-add-water kind.

"Why do you have to stir it so much?" I asked.

"So it doesn't get lumpy."

"Can I flip them?"

"When it's time," she said. "Do me a favor and get the griddle set up?"

I got the griddle from the cabinet and cleared off a spot on the counter, plugged it in, and turned it on. Mom looked over at me. At some point she must have rubbed her nose because there was flour on the end of it. Her face had new lines on it and when she smiled it seemed fake—like it was trying to trick the world into thinking everything was okay.

We ate breakfast and then I went and got my stuff for school and hugged Mom good-bye and went to the bus stop. Budgie was there. He was wearing a red-and-black plaid hat with earflaps. One of the flaps was pulled up and he had a cell phone pressed against his ear. I couldn't believe it. Where'd he get a cell phone from? And who was he talking to this early in the morning? Pizza Jungle wasn't even open yet.

"Hey."

"I'm on the phone."

"Sorry."

"Dude, I'm on the phone!"

He turned a little bit away from me and covered his mouth with his hand so I couldn't hear him. I bet there wasn't even anybody on the other end. I bet he was fake-talking just so I would see he had a cell phone and think he was cool for having one. I didn't, though, and it would take a lot more than just a cell phone for me to change my mind. He took the phone from his ear and pressed a button and put the phone in the pocket of his coat.

"Where'd you get the phone?"

"My mom and dad got it for me," said Budgie. He had this expression on his face like he thought he was cool but the earflap of his hat was still up so it didn't really work.

"It's got apps on it and everything."

"What're apps?"

"They're things that do stuff," said Budgie. "Jeez, don't you know anything?"

"I know things."

"No you don't."

"I do. I know lotsa things."

"Name one."

"I know the rubber sheets on your bed aren't so it'll be more comfortable like you said."

Budgie suddenly stopped trying to seem cool. Now he looked kinda nervous.

"Who told you that?"

"I asked my mom for some and she told me."

"Why? Why? Why would you ask for some?"

"My bed's uncomfortable sometimes," I said. "I also

thought if I had rubber sheets it'd be more like a trampoline."

Budgie swallowed. He opened his mouth like he was going to say something but then he closed it, digging into his pocket instead. He brought out his cell phone, stood next to me, and held it so I could see it. Then he showed me what apps it had and what they did. They were mostly games. There was a race car one and one where you shot chickens from a cannon. There were others, too. We played them on the bus all the way to school.

That morning was good. Me and Budgie played together at recess and we sat at the same table during lunch. We were even on the same dodgeball team during gym class. It was good to be on Budgie's team. He might not have been the best player but he threw the ball harder than anyone else. He even told me that one time he threw the ball so hard it knocked a kid out. I wasn't sure I believed that part but I was glad I was on his team so I wouldn't have to find out the hard way. Our team won three games to none and for a while everything was awesome.

It was after school at rehearsal when things started to be not so awesome. Mr. Putnam had Missy Sprout and Budgie and the rest of the helpers sit onstage while he did the roll call, and me, Violet, and the rest of the cast sat in the audience. Budgie'd lent me his cell phone and I was playing a game with the sound off and even though I was only listening to Mr. Putnam with half an ear I heard him call Budgie's name. Then Mr. Putnam asked Budgie something from so far out of left field it made me stop playing and look up. In fact it made everyone stop and look up.

"So Budgie," he said. "Were you named after the Duke?"

"Who's the Duke?"

"You've never heard of the Duke? John Wayne?"

"My name's not John."

"John wasn't his real name either," said Mr. Putnam. "It was Marion. Like yours."

I felt the color drop out of my face and I could see Budgie swallow from where I was sitting in the third row. Some of the kids onstage started to whisper to each other and giggle. Budgie licked his lips nervously.

"How did you—?"

Then his eyes fell on me and suddenly he didn't seem so nervous anymore. I'll say one thing about Budgie—for an idiot he could be awfully smart sometimes. This was big. And I didn't think he would care that I didn't really do it or that I had tried to fix it. Even though it was his parents who'd named him Marion, the way *he* would see it, I was the one who who'd let the cat out of the bag.

He sat onstage and stared at me like I was the only one in the room. His face had gone red and if he were a cartoon there would be smoke shooting from his ears. I sank down into my seat. How was I supposed to know Mr. Putnam knew of the only other guy in the world named Marion? It wasn't fair that my day was being ruined by somebody I'd never heard of.

For the rest of the afternoon I kept expecting Budgie to do something for revenge but he didn't. Mr. Putnam had him looking through the script and copying stuff onto a big piece of paper with a Magic Marker. I felt bad. I'd already heard a few whispered Marions, a couple of Mary Annes and even one Marilyn. I could have made a big scene and told everyone to cut it out but I was afraid that might make things worse. After rehearsal Budgie grabbed all his stuff and left quickly. Phoebe must have been right there waiting for him because by the time I'd gotten out to the turn-around in front he was gone.

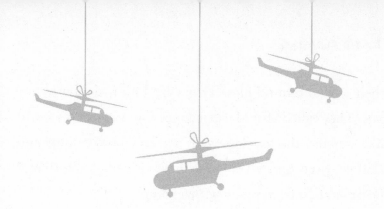

I HAD TROUBLE SLEEPING again that night. I still felt bad that Budgie had been embarrassed and that the next few weeks probably weren't going to go so great for him. I was pretty sure that by now the entire town knew what had happened and everybody, maybe even the grown-ups, were going to start calling him Marion.

Mom said if I felt bad, then I should say I was sorry and then it would be up to Budgie to forgive my mistake. I told her I didn't think he would. I told her that now he probably thought I was a bigger archenemy than before. She hadn't really known what to say about that, so I lay in bed for a long time wondering what was going to happen tomorrow—how Budgie would get his revenge and how many times he would get it.

But Budgie didn't do anything. Not in the morning at the bus stop. Not during recess or lunch or rehearsal or anything. I couldn't figure it out. I mean, I'm sure he hadn't forgotten about it and even if he had, people were sure doing their best to remind him. They called him Marion on the bus. They called him Marion at recess and lunch. It seemed like me and the teachers were the only ones calling him Budgie. Even Barely O'Donahue was getting in on it until he came back from recess with a fat lip.

Me and Budgie didn't walk to rehearsal together. We didn't sit together onstage while Mr. Putnam gave notes and made announcements. All day I'd been hoping for a chance to apologize to Budgie but there wasn't a time when he didn't seem like a jack-in-the-box half a crank from popping open.

It was the final dress rehearsal and everyone was in costume. Marley's ghost got to wear chains while I had buckles made of silver foil taped to my shoes. Chains were way cooler than fake buckles. Plus I was wearing knickers. Nobody said anything though. They were too busy making fun of Scrooge's nightshirt and cap.

Today's run-through was the last one in an empty auditorium. Tomorrow there would be people in the seats. Mom was going to be there. I wondered if she'd be in the front row. I wondered if I'd be able to see her. Mr. Putnam said he didn't want us looking for our parents and friends while we were onstage but I figured I could get away with one or two little peeks if I was sneaky enough.

Final dress rehearsal also meant full performance conditions with lights and props and no talking backstage or in the wings. It meant if you weren't in the scene or about to be in a scene you had to wait in the classroom across the hall until one of the backstage helpers came to get you.

I didn't think I'd need the backstage helpers, though. I knew exactly when I needed to be onstage. Also, Mom had switched her shift with someone at the hospital so she could be here so there was no way I'd miss my entrance.

"You're still coming to the play, right?"

"Of course I'm still coming," Mom said.

It was dinnertime. People had been stopping by the house since Saturday with food, and the fridge was full of stuff I'd never even heard of. Mom was heating a bowl full of something in the microwave.

"What's that stuff? It looks like brains."

"That's because it *is* brains."

"No way, really?"

"Not really," she said. "It's beef Stroganoff."

The microwave started beeping. Mom opened it and took out a Tupperware container full of noodles and brown stuff. Steam rose from it and I got the feeling it was trying to escape what was inside.

"What's that?"

"Y'know Hamburger Helper?" Mom asked.

"Yeah."

"Beef Stroganoff is Hamburger Helper's rich uncle."

I thought about that for a minute and decided I'd try it. After all, I liked Hamburger Helper and even though I wasn't rich I definitely liked the idea of it. And as far as I could tell from TV, money made everything better. I ate a plate of the beef Stroganoff. It tasted all right but I still didn't ask for seconds. I wanted to make sure to leave room for dessert because someone had dropped off a chocolate cake.

After dinner I went to my room and sat at my desk and did my homework. Then I packed up my book bag and got ready for bed. I washed my face. I brushed my teeth. I rinsed with that fluoride stuff that was supposed to taste like grapes but wouldn't no matter how many they drew on the bottle.

Then I got in bed and pulled the covers up and looked up at the space where the Apache helicopter had been. After a little while, I got out of bed and went to look for my mom. I heard the shower going in the bathroom so I stood in the hallway and waited for her to be done. The shower turned off a few minutes later. A minute after that the door opened and she came out.

"Where's my helicopter?"

"Jesus, Derek! Don't do that!" she said. "You scared me half to death!"

She had her bathrobe on and her hair was wrapped in a towel. I could smell her soap.

"Why did you take my helicopter down?"

"I need a minute here, Derek. You almost gave me a heart attack."

"What did you do with it? Did you throw it away?"

"It's in the attic."

"Why?"

"Because I didn't think you'd want to be reminded of— of what happened to your father."

"But it's mine! You can't just go into my room and take stuff!"

"You're right. You're absolutely right, Derek, and I'm sorry. That was wrong of me."

"Go get it!"

"Are you sure?" she asked. "It won't give you bad dreams?"

"Why would it do that?" I said. "I'm not scared of Dad."

"Sad dreams, then. I think it would give me sad dreams."

"I'm not you."

Mom looked hurt all of a sudden. Her face scrunched

up as if she might cry and she pulled her bathrobe tight like she hoped it was armor or something, like my words would bounce off but they didn't. They stuck in her like arrows.

"Let me just—give me a minute to change."

Mom went into her bedroom and closed the door. I stayed in the hallway. I felt bad that I'd hurt Mom's feelings but I also felt kinda powerful. Maybe that's why Budgie did what he did and said the things he said—because he liked how it made him feel. I wanted to feel powerful, too, but not this way. I didn't want to be like Budgie. I could hear my mom crying in her room and I even took a step toward her room before turning around and going back to mine.

MY EYES FLEW OPEN at five-sixteen in the morning. I felt electric. I *thrummed*. My fingernails were even glowing, I swear. And it wasn't because Christmas was less than a week away, it was because tonight was opening night. Instead of dancing sugar plums, my head was filled with visions of red carpets and *paparazzi*. Violet was with me, on my arm, smiling and laughing. Her dress was a candy apple red.

I thought about how I'd bow during the curtain call. How low should I go? And should I include a dramatic arm sweep? And with those things on my mind—how was I going to catch all the flowers I knew would be thrown my way?—I also thought about the very real possibility that the audience might demand a speech so I started to put together a list of people to thank.

I went through the day with my head in the clouds and before I knew it there were only ten minutes until curtain and I was in costume. I looked around the room at everybody, at Scrooge and Cratchit, the ghosts and Violet and Tiny Tim. They seemed calm. I wondered if I seemed calm to them. I hoped I did but the butterflies that were once in my stomach had been eaten by things that were bigger and much more ferocious and I was pretty sure that if everybody was quiet they'd be able to hear them chewing.

When there were five minutes until curtain Scrooge and Cratchit left the green room to take their places onstage. I wondered again why Mr. Putnam called it the green room. It wasn't green. It was just a regular old classroom that happened to be across from the backstage door to the auditorium.

I wanted to sneak in and peek through the curtains to look for Mom. We hadn't said much to each other this morning and the little we did say had nothing to do with what had happened last night and I felt bad. I wondered if she felt bad, too. She probably did. My stomach flipped. The butterfly-eating beasts dug their claws in and hung on. What if she was still upset? What if she was so upset that she decided not to come?

Suddenly I had to know if she was out in the auditorium but the play had already started and there was nothing I could do. The house lights were down and the stage lights were up and if I tried to peek now I'd be seen by the entire audience. I'd simply have to wait. I chewed my fingernails. I tapped my foot. I kept picturing a completely full house except for an empty seat in the front row with a little white sign on it that said "Reserved for Annie Lamb" in fancy writing. It was driving me crazy.

It had to be my turn to go on now. It just had to be.

I crossed the hallway and slowly opened the backstage door. Budgie was standing just inside.

"Close the door, Lamb," he whispered loudly. "You're not on yet!"

"Are you sure?"

He pushed me back into the hallway and pulled the door closed behind him. I looked at him. He was wearing a dark blue sweatshirt and dark pants, which made his sneakers seem awfully white.

"Aren't you supposed to be wearing dark shoes?"

"Aren't you supposed to wait in the green room?"

"Yeah, but nobody came and I was getting nervous," I said. "I thought maybe you forgot."

"I didn't forget! It's not even the second scene, moron!"

"But—"

He gave me a shove and turned around and went backstage again. I didn't go back in the green room like I was supposed to. I paced the hallway instead. Back and forth.

Waiting. Budgie didn't come back out. Maybe he forgot. Then I started to think that maybe he was doing it on purpose—that this was his revenge for telling everyone his real name.

My heart didn't just drop. It *plummeted*.

That was it. That had to be it. It wouldn't matter if I forgot to let Violet lead me off or I didn't project enough because Budgie was going to make sure I missed my entrance altogether. I'd be humiliated. Mr. Putnam would be furious. It'd be the perfect revenge if it weren't about to happen to me.

I had to do something. I couldn't just stand there and let Budgie do this to me. I would have preferred anything to this—a wedgie, an Indian rope burn, or even the dreaded French cuff, but no. Leave it to Budgie to figure out a way to cause maximum embarrassment with the least amount of work. I went to the backstage door, cracked it, and peeked in. I expected somebody to be there but the wings were empty. If I was going to do something I had to do it now. Without stopping to think about it I slipped inside and carefully closed the door behind me.

I moved to a dark corner in the wings and stood like a statue. My heart slowly climbed up out of my shoes and I found that now that I was backstage I wasn't worried about missing my entrance anymore. I'd just stay here, listen to the play, and when it was time for me to go on I'd just go out and do my scene. I'd embrace Violet and remember to project. I'd let her lead me offstage into the wings and presto!—Budgie's plot would have been thwarted. It was actually kind of perfect.

I smiled in the dark, picturing Budgie gnashing his teeth, stomping his feet, and shaking his fists in frustration. In fact, I was so busy imagining that I almost didn't notice when he came back. He was standing at least as still as I was and if he hadn't moved I was pretty sure I wouldn't have seen him at all.

But Budgie wasn't gnashing his teeth or stomping his feet or even shaking his fists. What he *was* doing, and doing gloriously, was picking his nose. He was two knuckles in at least, digging with his finger so far up one nostril I was surprised it wasn't coming down the other side.

I blocked the laugh as it was coming out, clamping my hands over my mouth as hard as I could. My shoulders shook. I tried swallowing the laugh but that only made me have to burp. It literally felt like something was going to burst.

"You're not on yet!" Budgie hissed. "Get out of here!"

I wanted to answer him but was afraid of what sounds

would escape if I put my hands down so I shook my head instead.

"You idiot! You're going to wreck everything! Go back and wait in the green room!"

Budgie came at me like he was going to grab me but I didn't want to be grabbed. I didn't want to go back to the green room. I didn't even want to wait in the hallway. I tried to duck out of the way but there wasn't a whole lot of room and he got a handful of my shirt.

"Get off me!" I whispered as loud as I could.

"Shut up!"

"Let go!"

"Dork!"

"Moose!"

I made a fist, swung, and punched Budgie right in the eye. It was the first punch I'd ever thrown at an actual person. Budgie stumbled back a few steps, then stopped and looked at me. Something had changed. The world around us suddenly felt smaller. I looked at my hand still clenched into a fist at the end of my arm—this part of me, this *weapon* that I never knew I had had done something I never thought I was capable of. Budgie had made fists of his hands as well. Both of them.

"Wait, Budgie! I'm sorry! Budgie, wait—"

But he didn't.

His first punch hit me in the ear and my head sang with pain. Budgie just hit me, I thought. This is a fight. Holy crap, I'm in a fight! I threw up my hands in time to block the second punch but the third landed square in my gut and pushed all my air out. Then our legs tangled up and we toppled over backward and my head hit the floor so hard I saw stars. We rolled and I ended up on top of him. He wiggled underneath me, grabbing at my shirt, trying to throw me off. I held his wrists so he'd stop but he yanked one loose and punched me in the mouth.

"Stop! Hitting! Me!"

I struck him with each word. Then the dam burst and I couldn't have stopped even if I wanted to. At some point the cracks just became too wide and too numerous and I ran out of stuff to fill them with. Besides, in a strange, horrible way it felt good to let go. So I let go. And from my head to my heart to my hands it all came out.

My confusion and frustration about Budgie and why we weren't friends anymore caught him on the forehead. The trouble I couldn't seem to stay out of connected with his jaw. Everything I'd been keeping bottled up for so long—every cheek I'd turned and every time I'd held my tongue were a flurry of punches about his head. And finally, all of my anger and sadness, all of the unfairness that I'd been feeling, and all of the complete and total *suckiness* over what happened to my father, became a single blow—a hammer fist that found its way past Budgie's flailing hands and straight onto his nose.

There was a *crunch* and beneath my hand I could feel Budgie's nose shift.

I stopped. My breath whooped in and out and I could feel hot tears on my cheeks. It was suddenly very quiet. I slowly turned, shading my eyes from the spotlight that Budgie and I seemed to be in the middle of. I swallowed and lowered my hand. The auditorium was quiet. The spotlight was bright and hot and Budgie squirmed underneath me. I waved. Just a little.

"Hi, Mom."

That's when Budgie flipped me over and it started raining knuckles.

Teachers seemed to swarm in from everywhere. They came up from the audience. They seemed to spill from the wings. I think I even saw Señora Cruz drop from the ceiling on a rope like a commando. Budgie got pulled off of me. He was still kicking and thrashing, yelling words I don't think even grown-ups were supposed to know. I sat up and the room swam around me.

"Derek? Derek, are you okay?"

Mom. There suddenly. Holding me.

"Derek, honey? Oh, your poor face! Are you all right? Derek, say something."

"Ow."

Mom helped me stand and we walked offstage into the wings and through the backstage door. I leaned on her. My head hurt. I must have bitten my tongue when my head hit the floor because it was bleeding and now my mouth tasted like pennies. Also one of my teeth was loose. I wiggled it with my tongue.

"We're leaving. Where are your things?"

"We can't just—wait, why are *you* crying?"

"You were right about him, Derek. I'm sorry I ever—sorry I ever doubted you," she said, her voice catching a little. She took in a deep breath and let it out shakily. Her face was bright with tears and I could feel her arm trembling where it lay around my shoulders. She was holding it together. Barely. "Are your things in here?"

"What about the play? I didn't do my scene yet."

"You're hurt."

"But Mr. Putnam always says the show must go on."

"I hate to tell you this, honey, but I think it's going to have to go on without you."

"No!"

I stopped walking and ducked out from under her arm. I couldn't believe it. How could she do this? She knew how important this was to me. She'd even helped me put my costume together by turning an old pair of my pants into the knickers I was wearing. The silver foil buckles on my shoes had been her idea also. Now that I thought about it, she'd actually done more for the play than I had. I mean, all I did was memorize five words.

"Derek."

"No! I wanna go on! I wanna do it!"

"Come stand in the light. I need to check your pupils."

"Stop it!"

"But you're hurt."

"No I'm not!"

"Sweetheart, you're bleeding."

"So?"

"I'm just trying to protect you."

"From what? My life?"

"Yes. No. I don't know," said Mom. Tears ran down her face, slipping out each time she blinked. She tried to wipe them away with her hands but there were just too many. "All I know is that seeing you and Budgie up there fighting like that . . . it was awful. I was horrified. If I was any kind of mother I'd have done something so that it never would've happened in the first place."

"You couldn't have done that," I said.

"Why not?"

"Because nobody can see into the future."

"You're right. You can't see the future. That's why the world is a monster, Derek. It gets its teeth in you and just . . . shakes until—until there's nothing left. And a lot of times you don't even see it coming. Is it so wrong that I want to protect you from that—even a little?"

"I don't even know what you're talking about," I said. "What teeth?"

"Think of it this way," she said. "If you find a baby bear in the wild what should you not do?"

"Mess with it."

"And why is that?"

"Because the mama bear is probably close by."

"And?"

"Mama bears are very protective of their babies."

"Exactly," Mom said. She was crouched down in front of me and looking in my one good eye. The other one was pretty much closed from all the punching. "And right now the world is messing with my baby bear. So if I'm the mama bear, what am I going to do?"

"Rip the world's face off?"

"Yes, I—no. But what I *am* going to do is roar. This mama bear is going to roar so long and so loud the world will think twice before messing with you again. And I'm going to stand up and roar every time I think you're in danger no matter what it is or how old you are. The world makes us all grow up so fast and I just want . . . I want you to be a baby bear—*my* baby bear—for as long as you can, okay?"

"Okay."

"And I'm sorry for thinking you'd want to leave after what happened with Budgie back there. You're a lot tougher than I give you credit for sometimes. Your dad would be—well, he'd be very proud you didn't give up."

It hurt to smile but I didn't care.

"Derek, there you are. Are you okay?" said Mr. Putnam.

"My mouth tastes like pennies."

"How are they?"

"Okay I guess."

"You must be Derek's mother," he said, putting his hand out. "I'm John Putnam."

"Annie Lamb."

"Pleased to meet you, Annie. Would you mind if I borrowed Derek for a little while? We're going to take a mulligan and start again."

"But he's just been in a—yes. Yes, of course. Borrow away." Mom hugged me tight and kissed my cheek and smiled, whispering in my ear, "Good luck, baby bear."

"Actors don't say 'good luck,' Mom."

"Oh, they don't, do they?"

"No. They say, 'Break a leg.'"

"Considering what just happened I'm not going to do that. Is there anything else you can say?"

"Dancers have been known to say, '*Merde*,'" said Mr. Putnam helpfully.

"What's that?" I asked.

"It's French," Mom said, giving Mr. Putnam a look.

"Does it mean good luck?"

"It means poop," said Mom.

I burst out laughing. I tried to stop because it hurt my face but I couldn't.

"He's all yours," said Mom.

She gave me another quick hug and told me she'd be in the front row. Then she went through the backstage door and into the theater. Mr. Putnam had me go back to the green room and this time I stayed until Missy Sprout came to get me. I took my place onstage. I said my lines. I embraced Violet and remembered to let her lead me off. I even sneaked a little wave to my mom as we disappeared into the wings.

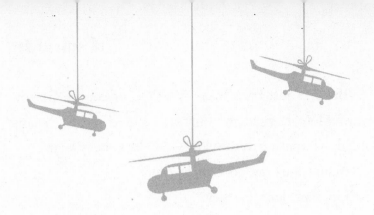

"WHO WAS YOUR FAVORITE person in the play?"

Me and M om were driving home. It was dark, and snow was blowing around outside the windows. I was still thinking about how Mr. Howard had come backstage after the play and when he was done congratulating everybody he took me aside. He told me he was proud of me and that I had showed a lot of character, pun intended. I beamed. I couldn't help it. Then he'd said we were going to have to talk about what had happened but not until after vacation. I still beamed. Only a little bit less. I fogged up the window with my breath and wrote my name in it.

"You were."

"I was?"

"Of course you were."

"What about Scrooge?"

"Didn't care for him."

"What about the ghosts?"

"Nope. No way. You were by far my favorite. It was really neat seeing you up there, Derek, and I'm so proud of you I could burst."

I smiled, looking out the window at the passing neighborhood. Christmas lights blinked in the trees and around front doors and along fences. Light-up icicles dangled from gutters. Robot Santas waved from front yards. In one yard, the two deer I thought for sure were fake suddenly bolted away when the garage door opened and light splashed out into the driveway. They were beautiful, crossing the next-door neighbor's yard in three big leaps and disappearing into the woods. My heart raced. I'd seen deer at the zoo before but this was way better. I was still thinking about them when Mom pulled into our driveway a few minutes later.

"Notice anything different?" asked Mom as she turned off the car.

"No, I—hey, you put lights up!"

They blinked and winked in the bushes next to the door and they flashed where they wound up the light post. The last time my dad was home for Christmas he'd gotten up on a ladder and run colored lights all along the gutters as well. That was a couple years ago though, and because Mom was afraid of heights we hadn't had them up there since.

I stood in the driveway and stared at the gutters, trying to remember exactly how they had looked all lit up for Christmas but I couldn't—at least not exactly. I pulled my coat tight and shivered. My mom was standing next to me and I could tell by the way her head was tilted that she was looking at the darkened gutters, too.

"Your lights look nice, Mom."

She looked down at me and smiled and put her arm around my shoulders. We stood like that in the driveway in the cold and looked at them until Aunt Josie opened the door and called us crazy for being outside for so long.

"Oh my God, Derek, what happened to your eye?" Aunt Josie asked once she saw my face.

"Me and Budgie threw down."

"Threw what down?"

"Nothing. We got in a fight. Y'know—threw down? Like they say on TV?"

"Oh, threw *down*. Of course. My bad," said Aunt Josie. "Are you okay? Do you want some meat for it?"

"Meat for what?"

"Your eye."

"Ew, no! Why would I want—how would I—no. No thanks."

"I think it's already done all the swelling it's going to do," Mom said. "Does it hurt when I do this?"

"*Ow!* What are you doing? Don't *touch* it!"

I jumped up from my seat and ran away a little, holding my hand over my eye for protection. Maybe it would be a good idea to get an eye patch. That way I'd have both hands free to defend myself.

"Sorry, sweetie!" Mom said. "I just wanted to feel if anything was broken. I *am* a nurse, remember?"

"Nothing's broken! It was fine until you started messing with it."

"How's your tongue?"

"What happened to his tongue?"

"He bit it."

"Now my mouth tastes like pennies," I said. "Also look!"

I wiggled the loose tooth with my tongue.

"Oh my God!" said Aunt Josie, cringing. "When did all this happen?"

"During act one. It's a baby tooth—see?"

I pulled my lip down and really wiggled it. Aunt Josie made a face and waved her hands like they were covered in spiders.

"Augh! Stop it!" she squealed. "Stopitstopitstopit!"

"What?"

"Loose teeth freak me out."

"Really? Why?"

"I don't know. They just give me the willies," she said, shuddering. "So please—for me—could you stop? Or am I going to have to turn my eyelids inside out?"

I stopped, *immediately* understanding what she was talking about. Loose teeth were one thing but turning your eyelids inside out? Now *that* was gross.

I helped Mom set the table. I put the plates out. I poured the milk. I even remembered which side the fork went on. Aunt Josie had made potatoes au gratin and green beans to go with the roast. I normally didn't like green beans but Aunt Josie had put crumbled-up bacon in them so they were okay. Sort of like the way broccoli was gross unless it was smothered in cheese. I wondered if the secret to cooking was just adding stuff you liked to stuff you didn't like.

Aunt Josie got the roast out of the oven and sliced pieces of it onto a plate and brought the plate to the table. Mom brought over the beans and potatoes and we all sat down. Nobody moved for a minute. Nobody said anything either. A big quiet dropped over the table like a blanket. Dad's chair had never seemed emptier.

"Have some wine with me, Jo?" Mom said.

She got up from the table and got a bottle from the rack. Then she dug through a drawer until she found a corkscrew and opened the bottle with it. She got two wine glasses from the cupboard, gave them a quick rinse, and brought them and the bottle back to the table.

I ate my dinner. Mom and Aunt Josie put food on their plates, too, but by the time I'd finished eating they'd barely started and I'd even had a second helping of potatoes. Nobody was really saying anything and the quiet was starting to drive me nuts.

"Do you think Santa will come this year?"

"Why wouldn't he? You've been good, haven't you?"

It felt like a trick question.

"I've been pretty good."

"I would say you've been *very* good, Derek," said Mom. "It's been tough and you've handled yourself well and I'm proud of you. You might not always use the good sense that God gave you but you *are* only eleven years old and sometimes eleven-year-olds just don't act the way you'd like them to."

"Thanks a lot."

"*But*," said Mom, holding up a finger, "your heart's in the right place, Derek. You're a good kid—a *great* kid. I can see it. Your aunt Josie can see it. Ms. Dickson can see it. And I'm pretty sure Santa can see it, too."

"When do you think he stops watching?"

"What do you mean?"

"I mean, he's got to load the sleigh and stuff."

"Are you worried he saw what happened today?"

"Yes."

"I hate to tell you this, Piggy, but he probably did. Don't freak out, though—Santa takes the whole year into consideration and not just the month between Thanksgiving and Christmas," said Mom. "And he doesn't load the sleigh, anyway—the elves do. It's a union thing."

I guess I knew that, too. I mean, I'd seen a lot of Christmas movies and it seemed like the elves did most of the work and Santa just stood around eating cookies and taking all the credit.

After dinner we decorated the tree. We strung lights all around it and hung ornaments from the branches and I got to stand on a chair and put the angel on top. When we were done decorating Aunt Josie turned the room lights off and the tree lights on and we all sat on the couch and looked at them for a while in silence. Snow was falling outside the windows and I was glad to be inside, safe and warm, snuggled between Mom and Aunt Josie. I could have stayed like that forever.

"What time is it?" I mumbled, feeling all fuzzy-headed and sleepy.

"Hm?"

Mom sounded like she was half-asleep. Aunt Josie was out completely. Her head was leaned back and her mouth was open and she was snoring.

"Time?"

"Hm? Oh . . . oh shoot! How'd it get to be nine thirty already?" she said, pushing herself up off the couch. "C'mon, c'mon. Let's brush teeth."

I rubbed my good eye, scratched my head, and yawned. Then I rose slowly and zombied through the kitchen and up the stairs to the bathroom. Mom had put my toothbrush on the sink for me. She was in her bedroom, probably putting her pajamas on.

"Where's the toothpaste?"

"Next to your toothbrush."

"Where's *my* toothpaste?"

"Just use mine."

"I like mine better," I said. "Mine tastes like bubble-gum."

"Please use mine."

"I'll just use the mouthwash instead."

"Derek, don't—wait! Do you hear that?"

"Hear what?"

"It sounded like an elf! Hurry! Brush your teeth and get in bed! Quick!"

I grabbed Mom's toothpaste, squeezed some onto my brush, and started brushing. It tasted awful. Thankfully, it wasn't in my mouth very long because I only brushed once in each direction before spitting it out. Then I ran down the hallway and into bed, kissing Mom good night as the quilt was still settling around me.

"Derek?"

"Yes?"

"Did you turn the water off?"

"Um . . . yes?" I said, pulling the quilt over my head.

"Derek."

"I forgot. Sorry."

"Don't worry I'll get it," Mom said. "Good night, sweetie. I love you."

"Love you, too." I fell asleep a little while later, listening hard for Santa's reconnaissance elves.

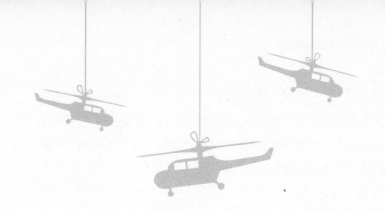

ON CHRISTMAS MORNING, I got out of bed, put on a sweatshirt and slippers, and snuck downstairs, careful not to wake Mom because it was still a little earlier than she would have liked. I peered around the doorway into the living room and in the dim light coming through the window could see Aunt Josie was asleep on the pull-out with one of those mask thingies over her eyes. Which meant I could plug in the tree without waking her. So I did.

I could see my stocking hanging from the mantel. It reminded me of something I saw on Adventure Kids once where they showed a python swallowing a goat, only instead of a leg sticking out of it there were candy canes, which was just as cool but in a totally different way.

I walked around the pullout to the fireplace, took down my stocking, sat on the floor, and dumped it out. Chocolate Santas and a bag full of tiny plastic ninjas tumbled into my lap. I held my stocking by the toe and shook it until a package of batteries and a couple of packs of Dinoboy cards fell out. There was something left in the stocking, though, so I stuck my hand in and grabbed it and wiggled it until it got loose. I pulled the package out and turned it over. It was an official Zeroman watch.

"Coooool."

The watch was encased in plastic and I turned it over and over in my hands, trying to figure out how to open it. I tried tearing it. I tried biting it. Nothing worked.

"Need some help?" Aunt Josie's voice made me jump. She was sitting up in bed with the mask thing pushed up on her forehead.

"Look! Look! Santa came!"

"I see that," said Aunt Josie. "Merry Christmas, kiddo."

"Merry Christmas!"

I climbed up onto the bed, gave her a giant hug, and dropped the package in her lap.

"Can you help me open this?"

Aunt Josie picked up the package, turned it over in her hands a couple times, and then pulled it apart. The watch fell out onto the bed and I scooped it up and strapped it on.

"Now open mine," she said. "It's under the tree."

I scrambled off the bed and found Aunt Josie's gift to me. It was a book. And its shape and weight suggested it was an educational one. I looked at Aunt Josie, hoping I didn't seem too disappointed.

"Don't worry," she said. "It's not a book."

"It's not?"

"It's a football."

"Really?"

She didn't have to tell me to stop being ridiculous. The look she gave me did that well enough. Maybe a little too well, actually.

"Just open it," she said.

I got back up on the bed and sat next to her. She put her arm around me and held me close as I removed the wrapping paper.

"He-ey, cooool!"

It *was* an educational book. But in the best way possible.

"Are there any presents left?" Mom asked from the doorway.

"Mom! Mom! Look what Aunt Josie got me! A book about samurais! Thanks, Aunt Josie!"

"You're welcome, Derek," said Aunt Josie. "I had a feeling you'd like it."

Mom sat down and then dragged me into her arms and hugged me. She was still warm from her bed and her hair smelled like sleep and dreams. We didn't let go of each other until Aunt Josie got out of bed a few minutes later and started rummaging around in the kitchen opening and closing the cabinets.

"Please tell me you're not out of coffee," she shouted.

"There's some in the pantry," said Mom. Then she saw the Zeroman watch I was wearing. "Ooh, what's that? Show me what that does."

I showed her all the stuff the watch could do.

"Wow," said Mom. "So how do you tell time on it?"

"What do you mean?"

"It's a watch, right?"

"Yeah."

"So which button do you press to find out what time it is?"

"I don't know. I don't think it's that kind of watch."

Aunt Josie made her special French toast for breakfast and afterward we went back into the living room to open more presents. I knelt in front of the tree, picked one up, and tore into it. Time seemed to speed up. Things blurred. When I'd run out of presents, I stopped and slowly looked around. The room looked like a tornado had hit it. Mom and Aunt Josie sat on the couch, holding their coffees, watching me.

"What?"

"Nothing," said Aunt Josie. "I think you may have just broken some kind of fast Christmas record, that's all."

I nodded. Maybe later on I could call the world record

people and ask about it. The phone rang a little while later
while I was flipping through my samurai book and Mom
got up and went into the kitchen to answer it.

Then she came back to the living room with the coffee
pot and emptied it into Aunt Josie's mug with the phone
pinned between her ear and shoulder.

"After lunch should be fine, Helen," she was saying.
"We'll be here."

She said some other things, too, but she said them as
she was going back into the kitchen so I didn't really hear
her. Why was Budgie's mom calling? I bet it was about the
fight. I bet Budgie had lied and told her it was all my fault
and that he was totally innocent so now she wanted to come
over and get her licks in, too. I heard Mom hang up the
phone.

"Derek, that was Budgie's mom on the phone. They're
coming over for tea later."

"When?"

"Three o'clock."

"Why?"

"I guess Budgie has something he wants to say to you."

"What is it?"

"I don't know. She wouldn't say."

"Well I don't want to hear it."

Mom came back into the living room and sat down on the couch and looked at me. Her face told me she was carefully choosing each word before she put them all together and said them.

"What if it's good?" she asked. "You'd want to hear it if it was good, right?"

"The only good thing to come out of Budgie's mouth was the time he burped the alphabet all the way to Q."

"That's disgusting."

"You shoulda been there. It even smelled like fish sticks."

"Ew, that's—why are you laughing?"

"I'm not!"

But I was. I totally was. I tried to stop but I kept thinking about that day and how Missy Sprout's face had gone green and she'd almost passed out and the more I thought about it the harder I laughed. Mom sat back on the couch and folded her arms.

"Whenever you're ready," she said.

Her mouth was trying to be serious but the rest of her face was laughing. We probably could've laughed longer but I got a bad case of the hiccups and had to stop because Budgie said that if you hiccup and laugh at the same time your lungs can come out of your mouth. Seriously. He'd seen it on the news and everything.

"They're coming at three?" asked Aunt Josie. "Derek, what time is it now?"

"I don't know."

"You're wearing a watch."

"It's not that kind of watch."

"What kind of watch is it?"

"It's this kind."

I held up my wrist, pressed a button, and zapped Aunt Josie with the laser beam.

The doorbell rang at ten past three and I jumped off the couch and ran upstairs to my room and closed the door. I didn't care if what Budgie had to say *was* good. I didn't even care if it was *awesome*. Nothing he could say would change anything. I flopped onto my bed and stared up at the spot where the Apache helicopter used to be. I was determined to stay there until Mom came to get me. Even then I wasn't sure I'd go quietly. After a few minutes there was a knock at the door.

"Who is it?"

"Dude, just open up."

Budgie! What was he doing here? Mom was supposed to have been the one to come get me! Now I wouldn't be able to make Budgie wait in the kitchen or anything.

"I know you're in there. Your mom said."

"Leave a message after the beep."

"Stop being a dork and open the door!"

I wasn't sure why Budgie thought calling me a dork would get me to let him in but I went to the door anyway. I figured the sooner I let him in, the sooner I could show him out. I opened it a crack and peeked through.

"What?"

I tried to sound mean but then I saw his face and suddenly I didn't feel like being mean anymore. In fact, I didn't think I could be mean now if I wanted to. Even though most of Budgie's face had healed over the past few days, his nose still reminded me of a poisonous mushroom.

"So can I come in?" he asked. "I wanna show you something."

He held up his cell phone and wiggled it a little. I opened the door the rest of the way and he came in. His nose looked worse in the light of my bedroom. It was all bulgy and purple and in a weird way I hoped I looked just as bad. That way it would be fair. I was pretty sure I did. At least it felt like I did. Budgie sat on the bed and started pressing buttons on his phone.

"Did you have something to tell me?"

"Nope."

"But my mom said your mom said you did."

"Oh yeah." He sniffled a little, wiping his nose on his sweater sleeve and leaving a glistening trail. "Sorry."

"For what?"

"Y'know, for being mean. And stuff." His voice sounded funny—like he had a really bad cold. "Okay, it's downloading! C'mere! C'mere!"

I sat next to him and he held the phone so we could both see the screen. Some of Budgie's excitement must have rubbed off on me because I started to feel all tingly.

"What is it?"

"Hang on a sec."

My eyes were glued to the screen. I didn't want to blink because I was afraid I'd miss it. I held my breath.

"Okay, here it is!"

I let my breath out. I blinked my eyes. I hadn't been sure what to expect but it certainly wasn't what I was looking at now. I felt a little bit cheated.

"So what?" I said. "It's just somebody's stupid school play."

"It's not just any stupid school play—it's *our* stupid school play."

I looked more closely at the screen. Budgie was right. It *was* our play! I suddenly got a strange feeling in my stomach—like it was dropping into my shoes and climbing out of my throat at the same time. Onstage, Mr. Cratchit and the rest of his family were looking off toward the wings as if they'd heard something.

"Here it comes," said Budgie.

I didn't have to look at him to know he was smiling. I could hear it in his voice. I knew what was about to happen and it didn't seem like something to smile about. And when it did happen it was hard for me to watch.

I tried to pretend that the boy tumbling out onstage with Budgie wasn't me. I tried to pretend that it wasn't me punching Budgie over and over again as he tried to get up and that they weren't my tears shining in the spotlight. I just didn't try hard enough.

"Wanna see it again?" Budgie asked.

"No thanks."

"It's funny though, right?"

"Where did you get it?"

"My mom found it on online."

"How?"

"Barely's mom called and told her it was there. It's already gotten a whole bunch of hits. Dude, we're gonna be famous!"

"Wait, your mom didn't go see the play?"

"No," he said. His smile went away and he put the

phone down. "But it's not like I was in it or anything. Plus, it was mostly middle schoolers."

"So what?"

"Sew a button on your butt, that's what."

Normally that would have been hilarious. Budgie smiled a little. But quickly. Then it was gone.

"What about your dad?"

"He was at work."

"I don't get it," I said. "Why wouldn't your mom come see the play?"

Budgie's hands were in his lap. He played with his fingers like he didn't know what else to do with them. Then he mumbled something.

"What?"

"I disappointed her too much."

"What are you talking about?"

"Remember that time I said that your parents love you less and less each time you disappoint them?"

"Kinda."

Budgie looked at me. Then he looked back into his lap.

"I think I disappointed her too much."

"What do you mean?"

"Nothing. Forget it. I don't wanna talk about it."

He stood up and walked around the room. He looked at the posters on my walls. He touched the stuff on my desk.

He pretty much kept his back to me the whole time. A few minutes went by and neither of us said anything.

"My parents don't love me anymore," he said suddenly.

"That's not true! Parents *have* to love their kids. It's in the constitution or something."

"Oh yeah? Then why'd they hire Phoebe to look after me? It's not like they suddenly had more stuff to do! They just don't want to deal with me anymore. Mom even said."

"What? No way!"

"Yes way! She's always saying stuff like that," he said. Then in his mom voice he added, "'Marion, I can't deal with you right now! Marion, I'm all done with you!'"

"What does your dad say?"

"He's never around."

"Where is he?"

"I mean, he's around. He's just—he gets up and goes to work and he comes home and he goes to his office. I'm stuck with Phoebe."

"What's so bad about her?"

"She writes poems and won't stop reading them to me."

"So?"

"They're *poems*."

He flopped into my chair and put his face in his hands. I had a feeling it wasn't really about Phoebe—not about her poems anyway. I wanted to make him feel better but didn't know how. People had given us food when they knew we were sad. I wondered if I should make him a sandwich or something.

"I wish my dad was more like your dad," said Budgie.

"Dead?"

It was the first time I'd said it out loud. I hated the way it sounded and how it felt in my mouth.

"No, not—not like that. I mean, *around*. Like your dad was."

"But he wasn't."

"Not all the time, I know, but when he was here he was *here*."

"Your dad's here."

"It's not the same," Budgie said. I could tell he was getting frustrated. His fists were clenching up and he was having trouble getting his words out. "My dad's here, yeah, but it's *like* he's not. With your dad, even when he was away it was almost like he was still here."

"What are you talking about?"

"Do you still have that lunch box with all your dad's letters?"

"Yeah."

"Can I see it?"

I got the lunch box out from under the bed and opened it. A few envelopes slid out onto the quilt. It was packed pretty tight after all. Budgie frowned.

"How many?"

"Ninety-one," I said. Then I told him that my dad tried to write every week but he couldn't sometimes because sometimes he was just too busy. I don't know why I'd added that part though. It seemed a little bit like rubbing it in.

Budgie sat down on the bed and pulled the lunch box into his lap. He took a deep breath and for a second I was worried he might lose his temper and take the letters and rip them up. I'd seen him do stuff like that when he got upset.

"And you wrote to him, too?"

"Yeah. All the time."

"Do you think he had a lunch box?"

"I'm not sure. I know he had a footlocker. Maybe he kept them in there."

"That's what I'm talking about."

"Footlockers?"

"Not footlockers, dorkus, the letters. Your dad was like a million miles away and you still knew what he was doing and he still knew what you were doing. My dad's just down the hall and I don't think he even knows my middle name."

"It's Cornelius, right?"

Budgie must not have heard me because he didn't do anything. Normally he would have given me a dead arm for saying his middle name out loud. He said something else then but I missed it.

"What did you say?"

"I said, Mom even thought we were still best friends until she saw the video clip."

"Wait," I said, "we're not best friends anymore?"

Budgie stopped. He picked up the letters that had fallen out of the lunch box and put them back in and closed the lid.

"I think maybe we're still friends," he said finally, "just not *best* friends."

It hurt to hear him say it even though I'd sorta known it was true for a while now. I still had a fuzzy memory of the first time we met—Budgie peeking from under his mom's skirt, afraid to come out and play. It wasn't fair how so much could change so fast.

"Why not?" I asked before realizing I might not like the answer.

Budgie shrugged. He was fiddling with his fingers in his lap again and when he finally picked his head up he didn't look me in the eye. He looked somewhere over my shoulder instead. Then he kinda glanced at my face before looking down into his lap again.

"I don't know."

"Did *I* do something?"

"No."

"So you're mean to me for no reason?"

"No!"

"Then why?"

Budgie lifted his head and looked me in the eye. He took a deep breath and let it out through his nose.

"Because you're . . . people say you're, y'know . . . weird."

"What? No way! I'm not—why? Why would they say that?"

There was plenty more I *could've* said—like just because somebody says something doesn't make it true or that thing about opinions being like buttholes because everyone had one and most of them stunk. I couldn't get the words to line up right in my head though. I just stared at Budgie with my mouth open for a second before I started to feel like a fish and closed it. *Me? Weird?*

"I don't know, I—look around you. Model airplanes? All your superhero dolls?"

"They're *action* figures!"

"Dinoboy, then. I mean, how old *are* you?"

"*You* like Dinoboy!"

"I *liked* Dinoboy," said Budgie. "In *third* grade! We're gonna be in middle school next year. *Middle* school. That's huge!"

"So you can't keep playing with that stuff."

"Because we're not *freakin'* kids anymore!"

Budgie's words were a slap in the face. Whoever made up that line about "sticks and stones" must have been lying. Or deaf. This time it was my turn to look away.

"So?"

"So if I hang around you I'm afraid people will think I'm weird, too."

"That's stupid!" I blurted out. "Who cares what people think?"

"I do."

When the conversation started I'd felt bad for me but now I kinda felt bad for Budgie. I hadn't thought about it before but maybe he was the way he was because otherwise *he'd* be one of the ones to get picked on. After all, he was what my dad once jokingly called a "target-rich environment."

We sat on the bed. I didn't look at Budgie. Budgie didn't look at me. If I had a tick-tock clock in here you totally could have heard it. I didn't though. My clock was digital. I looked at my hands. Fiddled with my Zeroman watch. Made it beep.

"What's that?"

"It's a Zeroman watch," I said. "Santa brought it."

"Cool. Can I see it?"

Me and Budgie played in my room until we heard his mom calling from the bottom of the stairs. Budgie took off the Zeroman watch and handed it to me, rolling his eyes back so far I bet he could see his brain. Then he put on his coat, went and got his phone and stuck it in his pocket.

"Are you doing anything for vacation?" I asked.

"I don't think so."

"Me neither. Maybe if it snows some more we could go sledding. Y'know, if nobody else is around."

Budgie's mom called out again and I couldn't help picturing a cartoon hippo on the landing, bellowing up the stairs. I closed my mouth tight so I wouldn't laugh. It was hard though. The hippo had a polka dotted bow and lipstick and everything.

"I gotta go," Budgie said, zipping up his coat. "She sounds real mad."

He went to the door then stopped and turned around and put out his hand. It took three tries but we finally remembered all the parts to our complicated secret handshake. When we were done, me and Budgie stood there just kinda looking at each other.

"I'm sorry," he said.

"Yeah. Me too."

THE SUN SHONE BRIGHTLY and in the cemetery snow was melting. Mom wore sunglasses but I don't think it was because of the glare. At the church she'd gotten up in front of everyone and told stories about Dad until she started to cry and had to stop. She hadn't said anything since. Instead she held on to Dad's wallet with both hands in her lap, sitting up as straight as I'd ever seen her sit. She appeared to be looking at the minister but I couldn't tell if her eyes were open or closed. I wished I could close mine or look away or something but no matter how hard I tried I couldn't seem to take them off the hole in the ground.

Mom, Aunt Josie, and I sat in folding chairs near the edge of the grave along with Nanny, Pappy, and Gammy Jess. Everyone else kinda stood behind us. Budgie and his mom and dad were among them as well as some of Dad's cousins we hadn't seen for a long time. I also recognized some of Mom's friends and a couple of people she worked with at the hospital. Six of my dad's army friends in their dress uniforms carried the casket, taking careful steps in the snow so they wouldn't slip as they brought it over from the hearse.

Once the casket was in place the minister raised a hand above his head and whatever talking there had been came to a stop. Sunlight flashed off his glasses. Mom took my hand and held it tight. In her other hand she still held my dad's wallet.

"In the midst of life we are in death . . . " the minister began.

Mom's hand twitched. Her grip on my hand tightened. I wondered what she was thinking about—was she remembering Dad and the good times they'd had together or was she thinking about the new life she was now forced to begin without him? I didn't want to think about either of them, personally. If I did I'd probably start to cry and I got the feeling Mom needed me to be strong right now—which would've been a lot easier if I couldn't see my Dad's coffin being lowered into the ground.

". . . suffer us not, at our last hour, for any pains of death, to fall from thee."

The minister picked up a handful of dirt and as he tossed it in the hole I finally found the strength to close my eyes.

"In sure and certain hope of the resurrection to eternal life . . ."

Darkness. The scrape of shovels.

". . . we commend to Almighty God our brother Jason and we commit his body to the ground . . ."

Sobbing behind me. Mom's grip tightening on my hand.

". . . lift up his countenance upon him and give him peace . . ."

The minister paused. For some reason I held my breath. I don't know why.

". . . *Amen.*"

Me, Mom and Aunt Josie were the last ones to leave the cemetery because just about everyone stopped and said how sorry they were again and what a great guy they thought my dad was. Even though I liked hearing it I'd really had enough for one day. So had Mom. I could tell.

I looked through the back window of the car as Aunt Josie drove slowly through the gates to the main road and could see a mini loader chugging up the small hill toward my dad's gravesite. There was only one reason for it to be heading that way and I didn't want to think about it. I turned back around and faced the front. Neither Mom nor Aunt Josie were saying anything and I wasn't saying anything either. It had been silent in the car for so long that when Aunt Josie finally cleared her throat it was like a gunshot.

"That was a nice service, wasn't it?" she said.

"As nice as a funeral service can be, I suppose," Mom answered. Then she chuckled a little. "Jason would have said all the sad people really brought the place down."

"Like a trip to Dragsville, Ohio," I added.

"Or breakfast at the International House of Bummer."

"God, he could be *such* a dork sometimes," said Aunt Josie. "I mean, seriously? IHOB?"

Then it dawned on me—we were driving home after burying my father and we were all *laughing*. It didn't feel inappropriate. It wasn't disrespectful. It was exactly the opposite. And in a weird way I'd never felt better. We got some strange looks at a stop light and it wasn't until we'd driven away that I realized we hadn't yet taken the FUNERAL sign out of the window, which, for some reason, made us laugh harder. We were still giggling when we got home but it tapered off as we turned in from the street to find a car in our driveway.

Aunt Josie pulled in next to it and turned off the engine. I could see somebody in the driver's seat—a big somebody who didn't so much step from the car as *shrug* himself out of it like he was taking off an overcoat. Sunlight winked off the brass buttons and badges pinned to his jacket.

"Can I help you?"

"Annie Lamb?"

"Yes," Mom said. "And you are?"

"Sergeant Jahri Glover, ma'am," said the soldier. "I served with your husband and came to offer my condolences."

"Thank you, Sergeant. Can I interest you in a cup of coffee?"

Mom unlocked the front door while Sergeant Glover leaned back into his car and got a big manila envelope from the passenger seat. He saw me when he straightened up and seemed to be studying me as he pushed the car door closed.

"You're Derek," he said.

I nodded.

"It's so good to finally meet you. My name's Jahri."

He put his hand out and when I took it mine disappeared completely. Seriously. It looked like my arm ended at the wrist.

"It's good to meet you, too," I said. "You knew my dad?"

"Sure did. Hey, your mom said something about a cup of coffee—mind if we go inside and see about it?"

Jahri took his hat off and was careful to wipe his shoes on the mat when we came in. I kicked mine off and went into the kitchen. I hadn't been hungry lately but now that the funeral was over and everybody had said what they'd come to say my appetite had returned. And not a moment too soon—Mom had just put a plate of cookies out on the table. Her voice stopped me as I reached for one.

"Derek, don't be rude," Mom said. Her back was turned and she was getting coffee mugs down from the cabinet. "Offer the cookies to Sergeant Glover first."

"His name's Jahri, Mom."

"Oh, is it?"

"It's all right," he said. "I prefer it, actually."

"The coffee will be another minute but please have a seat and help yourself to some cookies."

Jahri pulled out a chair and sat down, putting the manila envelope on the table. It bulged. Full of something. I sat down across from him and waited for him to take a cookie. He was looking at me—studying me again the way he had in the driveway.

"You should have a cookie," I said. "They're awesome. Really."

He smiled and reached for the plate. Then he seemed to have second thoughts and sat back again.

"What?" I said. There was something in the way he was looking at me that made me want to tell him everything I'd ever done. Mom came around and put coffee mugs, a little thing of milk, and the sugar bowl on the table. Jahri turned around in his chair.

"Can I help with something?" he asked.

"No. Please sit. The coffee's nearly—see? There we are."

Mom grabbed the coffeepot before the machine had even stopped beeping. She filled Jahri's mug first, then Aunt Josie's, and then her own. Jahri thanked my mom and blew on his coffee before taking a sip.

"Derek," he said as he put the mug down, "would it be okay with you if I talked with your mom for a little while? Why don't you go to your room and I'll come find you when we're done, cool?"

"Yeah. Cool. Totally."

"Let me put you out your misery first, though," he said, smiling again and taking a cookie from the plate. He put his fist out as I went by and I bumped it with one of mine. Of course I had to shift a few cookies in order to do so. "See you in a little while, partner."

I must have dozed off waiting for Mom and Jahri to finish talking because the next thing I remembered was a knock on my bedroom door. There were cookie crumbs between the pages of the comic book that lay open on my chest. I took it to the wastebasket and shook the crumbs into it because I didn't want to attract mice. Mom once told me that she and Dad had had another son before me but that he kept eating chips and stuff in the bedroom and never cleaned and that the crumbs attracted mice and then one night the mice carried him away and they never saw him again. And as crazy and impossible as that sounded, I wasn't about to take any chances.

"Derek?" said Jahri's voice in the hall. "You good?"

"I'm good."

"Can I come in?"

"Yeah. Yes," I said.

Jahri came in and my room suddenly seemed a lot smaller. He didn't sit right away. Instead he walked slowly around the room looking carefully at everything, ducking occasionally to avoid running into a model airplane. Putting the big envelope on my desk, he sat in my chair and studied me again for a moment before speaking.

"Has anyone ever told you that you look just like your daddy?"

"Yeah, I guess."

"Naw, I mean *just* like him. I seen pictures and everything but . . . damn. How old are you now? Ten?"

"Eleven," I said. "My birthday's in October."

"That's right," he said, shaking his head. "Sorry for staring. It's just I keep expecting his voice to come out your mouth. I ain't going to lie, Derek, there's not a whole lot of truly good people out there—and Lord knows I ain't one of them—but your daddy definitely was. Something about being around him just made you *feel* good. Made you happy. A lo-ot of people going to miss him."

I didn't say anything and for a minute Jahri didn't either. Then he reached back and got the envelope and handed it to me. Whatever was inside shifted a little. Rustling.

"He loved these but I think he would've wanted you to have them."

"What are they?"

Jahri shrugged.

"Open it," he said. "They're yours after all."

I fumbled with the envelope's clasp with fingers that suddenly wouldn't stop trembling. *They're yours after all?* What did that mean? I couldn't think of anything my dad might have had that belonged to me. Finally I got the clasp undone and I folded the flap back and shook the envelope out.

Letters. My letters. Tumbling out onto the comforter. The different years bundled together with rubber bands. I recognized my mom's handwriting on the outsides of the early ones before my own was readable to anyone but her, back when I wasn't that good at writing and told her what to write instead. Back when I drew pictures. I sifted through the envelopes, seeing my penmanship get better with each one, watching myself grow up in the alphabet.

When I looked up at Jahri he was blurry.

"You okay?"

I nodded. A knot was rising in my throat and any words I might have said would have been trapped behind it. I was afraid that if I opened my mouth I'd start crying and never be able to stop.

"This is yours, too," said Jahri.

I took the laminated strip of construction paper from him and unfolded it. It was creased and a little faded and at first I had no idea what I was looking at. Then I recognized my scribbling. It must have been from when I was in first grade or something—two stick figures drawn in peach-colored crayon with dandelion zigzags for hair and brick red smiles so big they went outside the lines. The taller figure was holding the smaller one's hand and "ILOVYUDADDREK" was scrawled underneath, the letters all squished together because I hadn't given myself enough space to write. I stared at the picture for a long time, trying to remember having drawn it but it was just too long ago and I couldn't. Not even a little.

"He told me that bookmark was the first present you ever gave him. It was for father's day," said Jahri. "He kept it in his boot."

"I don't remember."

"That's okay. Now you will."

"What if I don't? What if I forget him?"

"I don't think that'll happen."

I swallowed hard and spoke carefully. When the words came out they were shaky and quiet.

"I'm afraid it already has."

"Naw."

"It has," I said. "All day today. No matter how hard I tried I couldn't remember what he looked like or what he sounded like. Why can't I remember?"

"You going through a tough time now, Derek. A *real* tough time. Things are going to be different for a while. But they'll be normal again."

"Everyone's been saying that."

"That's because it's the truth," said Jahri. "You'll remember. Soon enough. You'll see."

He hung out in my room with me and we shot the breeze for a little while. Jahri asked me how my Christmas was and how school was going and I asked him a few questions as well—where was he from? Charlottesville, Virginia. Did he have any kids? No. When I asked him if he'd ever shot anyone he told me that sometimes his job required it. He wouldn't say any more about it and I didn't ask. A little while after that he said he had to go so I walked downstairs with him where he said good-bye to my mom and out onto the porch where he and I shook hands again. I stayed there, leaning on the rail as he walked to his car.

"Thanks," I blurted suddenly. Jahri stopped and turned around. "Y'know, for bringing the letters back. And the bookmark. I really—I just—thank you."

"You're welcome, Derek. Your daddy would have done the same for me. For anybody really. He was something else, your daddy was, and I truly hate that he's gone."

He paused then, studying me. After a moment he shook his head a little and smiled.

"You worried you can't remember him? Son, just look in the mirror. For real."

Then he saluted sharply, kinda folded himself down into the car, and drove away.

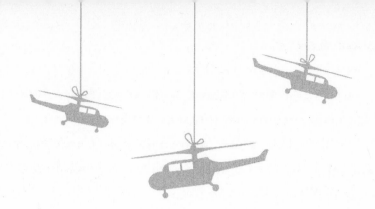

THE NEXT DAY WAS just a normal day in the week with nothing really to look forward to. It was too late to say "Merry Christmas" and too soon to start wishing people "Happy New Year." Then Mom stuck a list on the fridge of the thank-you notes I had to write. That was it. The holiday was officially over.

I sat at my desk with the list in front of me having already done everything I could think of to avoid actually writing them. I'd shoved some stuff around in my closet to make room for other stuff. I'd made my bed. I'd even put my dirty clothes in the hamper and the pile of clean clothes away in the dresser. At least I thought they were clean. There was actually a pretty good chance I'd gotten it backward.

"Derek, how are those thank-you notes coming?" Mom called from the bottom of the stairs.

"Good!"

"Are they finished?"

I looked at the thank-you card on my desk. I hadn't written any words yet. Instead I'd drawn a cool superhero called Future Boy who could time travel, which was funny considering that particular ability would really come in handy right about now.

"Um . . . almost?"

I heard Mom coming up the stairs. Then I heard her footsteps in the hallway. Then I heard her knock on my door.

"Wait! Wait! Don't come in yet," I said, shifting Future Boy to the bottom of the blank thank-you card pile so Mom wouldn't see him. "Close your eyes first!"

"Why?"

"I have a surprise!"

"Are your thank-you notes done? Is that the surprise?"

"You'll see. Just close your eyes."

"Okay. They're closed. I'm coming in now."

The door opened slowly and I saw Mom standing there with her eyes scrunched tight. She walked a few steps into the room and then stopped. If she went up on her tiptoes her head would touch my model of the Hawker Hurricane. I counted to three and Mom opened her eyes.

"Hey! Who picked up your room?"

"I did!"

"So who's been writing your thank-you notes?"

"Mo-om!"

"Sorry. It was good of you to clean up. And as a reward—here," she said, handing me a bunch of envelopes and a sheet of stamps. "I wrote the addresses on them so you don't have to. Could you just stamp them and run them out to the mailbox when you're done?"

"Why can't you do it?"

"Because I have to run a few errands before work."

"Couldn't you just drop them off at the post office? That's an errand, right?"

"I could if they were finished," she said, taking a step forward. I quickly scooted my chair between Mom and the blank cards on my desk. "Are they finished?"

"Why don't I just take them out when I'm done?"

"Good thinking. Remember—the mailman gets here around one thirty so they'll need to be in the mailbox before then, okay?"

I looked at my clock. It was noon. I was going to have to work fast. Mom hugged me good-bye and I spun my chair around, grabbed my pencil, and, after finishing the hero I'd been drawing, started writing.

My hand cramped after a little while but I kept going. The eraser was hard and didn't really work but I didn't let that stop me. I thanked people for this. I thanked them for that. My hand was a blur. Smoke rose from the tip of my pencil. If there was a superhero with special thank-you-note-writing powers, it would definitely be me. All I needed was a cape.

I signed my name to the last card and put my pencil down. My hand throbbed. My back hurt from being bent over for so long and I was tired. But I was done. This is how Hercules must have felt after finishing all those tasks—I was sure of it.

I slid the notes into the envelopes, licked them shut and put stamps on them. Luckily, they were the self-sticking kind. My tongue couldn't take any more of the glue. I made a small stack of the envelopes and spun my chair around and looked out my window just in time to see the mail truck pulling up next door.

It was twelve forty-three. The mailman was early.

I scooped up the envelopes, bolted down the stairs and out the door. I didn't stop to put a jacket on. I didn't even stop for shoes. Pebbles dug into my feet as I pounded up the driveway, hollering and waving the thank-you notes in the air. I caught the mailman's attention as he pulled up to our mailbox and as I slowed from a run to a walk I tripped and me and the thank-you notes went flying.

I hit the ground, rolled, and ended up on my back. The driveway was hard and cold. The sky overhead was gray. A few snowflakes drifted down around me. I didn't think I was hurt but I did feel a little embarrassed so when I heard the mailman's voice I covered my face with my hands.

"You all right, kid? That was some digger."

"I'm okay."

"Are you sure? Let me see your face."

I dropped my hands. The mailman was standing over me. He wore a hat with earflaps and had a big mustache. I could see his breath as it puffed out of him. His knees crackled as he crouched next to me.

"I'm fine," I said. "See?"

"No you're not. You're all banged up."

"I was like this before I tripped."

The mailman looked at me like he thought I was crazy and shook his head a little. Then he helped me up and together we collected the thank-you notes that had been scattered around the driveway. One of them had blown into the yard and I went and got it and brought it to the truck where the mailman was waiting with our mail.

"You should run along inside now. It's cold out here," he said, handing me a bunch of letters that were held together with a red rubber band. "And, kid?"

"Yeah?"

"Watch your step."

Then he slid the door shut, waved at me through the window, and pulled away. I turned and headed back to the house, taking the rubber band off the letters and flipping through them. I skipped a few though because I was starting to not feel my fingers. The mailman had been right—it *was* cold. I hadn't noticed it at first but now it had gotten so far inside of me it felt like my bones were made of ice. I stuck the mail under my arm and breathed into my hands as I hurried to the front door, which I had accidentally left open.

I ran up the steps, pulled the door closed, and tossed the mail onto the kitchen table on my way to the living room where the fire was. I plopped down in front of the fireplace and stuck my hands out, letting the heat chase some of the cold out of me. If there were a way to take a few of the flames and rub them on me to warm up faster I totally would have done it. If I could have sat right in the fire I would have. I was that cold all of a sudden. I heard Aunt Josie come down the stairs and into the kitchen.

"It's freezing in here! Is the door open?"

"I went out and got the mail," I said. "I might not have closed it all the way."

"You need to make sure, okay? Listen for the click. If you don't hear the click, then the door isn't . . . um . . . Derek?"

"Yeah?"

"You have some mail here."

"What is it?"

I didn't want to move from my spot in front of the fire. I was warm now, hot even. My cheeks were like embers. I felt like I was glowing. Behind me Aunt Josie coughed a little to clear her throat.

"Sweetheart, it's from your dad."

I SAT ON MY BED. The envelope was on the quilt in front of me. Unopened.

I wasn't warm anymore but I wasn't cold either. Part of me really, really wanted to read the letter but another part of me almost wished it hadn't come. I picked up the envelope and looked at my name spelled out in Dad's blocky handwriting—the letters kinda ran into each other even though it wasn't exactly cursive. I ran my finger over it and could feel each letter where it had been pressed into the paper as if it was some kind of reverse braille.

I held it to my nose and sniffed. It smelled like the ninety-one other envelopes in the Knight Rider lunch box under my bed. The only thing different about it was that it was the last one. I wondered if Dad had known somewhere deep down inside that he'd never be writing to me again. And if he did know—had it changed what he put in the letter? I wondered what I'd write if I knew they were going to be my last words. It'd be something heroic, probably.

I didn't know what to do. If I opened the letter, then that would be it. I'd have the last words Dad had ever written and they'd say what they said even if it was just a bunch of knock-knock jokes or a grocery list or something. On the other hand, if I didn't open the letter, it could say whatever I wanted it to say. It could say what I needed it to say. For as long as I needed it to say it.

"Derek, sweetheart, is everything okay?"

It felt weird talking to Mom while she was at work. Maybe it was because I wasn't supposed to call her there. I heard beeping in the background and pictured her at the nurse's station, talking into her cell phone while people with tubes sticking out of them stumbled around asking for medicine.

"Yeah, everything's fine. Hey, what's that beeping sound?"

"I can't really talk now, sweetie, what is it?"

"I finished the thank-you notes."

"That's it?"

"Yeah, and I brought them out to the mailbox like you said. Did you know our mailman has a mustache?"

"Derek."

"A really big one."

"Derek, listen, I really can't—"

"I got a letter from Dad."

The beeping in the background suddenly seemed louder. I could even hear the sound of the intercom even though I couldn't understand what it was saying. Mom hadn't said anything for a while and her silence was starting to scare me a little. I hoped I hadn't disappointed her.

"Mom? Hello?"

"What did it say?"

"I don't know. I haven't opened it yet."

"Why not?"

I told her everything that I'd been thinking about. Mom listened without saying anything.

"Is that weird?" I asked when I was finished. "Am I weird?"

"No, of course you're not weird. Why would you think that?"

"I don't think most people think the same way I do. Most people would just open the letter."

"You're not most people, Derek, and y'know what? I'm glad you're not most people. Sometimes it's better *not* to do what everyone else is doing. Take lemmings for example—" She stopped and took a breath. "The important thing—the *only* thing really—is how you see yourself. In the end, that's all that matters. Opening the letter is your decision, okay? And I won't think you're weird if you decide not to."

I thought about that for a second, picturing hundreds of lemmings as they charged over a cliff into the ocean except for one that was struggling to go in the other direction.

"I think I'm going to open it," I said. "But not because it's what everybody else would do. It's what *I* want to do."

"Good."

"Plus Dad may have included some special, secret army codes for me to crack, you never know."

"No you don't, do you?" Mom said. "I hate to say this but I have to go now. Are you going to be okay?"

I pictured the lemming again. It wasn't any bigger or stronger than the rest but it kept going no matter how many times it got pushed back or run over.

"Yeah, Mom. I will. I'll be okay."

She hung up and I hung up and I sat there on her bed for a minute not feeling like I might be weird anymore. And so what if I was? If people thought I was weird that was their problem. I got up, went to my room, and tore the envelope open, but when I shook it to get the letter out a picture fell out instead.

My dad. In his flight suit. His helmet under one arm. Smiling. Giving the thumbs-up. The sun glinted off his sunglasses. The Apache helicopter was a ginormous black hornet behind him. I remembered this one time Dad told me that the ground troops always said they felt safer when they heard an Apache overhead. Now I knew why.

I looked at the picture for a little while. Then I turned it over to see if he'd written anything on the back but he hadn't so I put it aside and slid the letter out of the envelope. I hadn't taken a breath in what seemed like a long time. For some reason the letter was trembling as I unfolded it.

> *Derek—*
>
> *Guess who's not grounded anymore?*
>
> *I'll be flying a sortie in a little while and wanted to write before I left to wish you good luck in your play. I'm sorry I won't be there to see it. I know you'll be great and I'm proud of you for trying something new (even if it's only because there's ghosts in it).*
>
> *I was sorry to hear from Mom that Budgie's giving you some trouble. I bet she's telling you to be the bigger person, right? It's a good idea but honestly, an idea won't stop him from bugging you. Don't give up though—every problem has a solution, even if it's not clear at first. You'll find it.*

*Zeroman sounds really cool. I can't wait to
watch it with you. It might not be for a little
while, though, so you'll have to fill me in on all
the details when I get home, O.K.?*
Love,
Dad
*P.S. How do you like my chopper? Her name's
Buttercup.*

When I finished reading it I read it again. I studied the
way each letter ran into the next, the way his *n*'s sometimes
looked like *h*'s and how there were some letters that didn't
look like letters at all but were weird squiggles instead and
the only way to figure out what he meant was by reading
the stuff around it. I had joked with Mom about it but
Dad's letters really *were* written in a kind of code. It was
just a code I'd gotten used to cracking.

I put the letter and the picture back into the envelope
and put the envelope under my pillow. Then I lay back with
my hands behind my head and stared up at the hook where
my Apache helicopter used to hang. Maybe it was because
it was directly overhead or maybe it was because it was the
only spot on my ceiling that didn't have a model hanging
from it but the empty space seemed huge. If it were a voice,

it'd be yelling. I didn't like being yelled at.

I got up, went to the linen closet, and found the hook-ended stick we used to pull down the attic stairs, reminding myself to get out of the way this time. The door *sproinged* downward and the steps came clattering out.

"Derek!" Aunt Josie called from downstairs. "Are you okay? What was that?"

"Nothing!" I shouted back. "I'm just getting something from the attic!"

"The attic? Why? What are you getting?"

But I was already halfway up the stairs and pretending I didn't hear her. It was cold in the attic and my breath came out of me in little clouds as I felt around for the pull string that would turn the light on. I almost went back down for a sweater but then my fingers brushed the string and I grabbed it and gave it a tug. The light came on, dim at first, but getting brighter as it warmed up and I watched the shadows retreat into the corners. I wasn't scared—I just hoped what I was looking for wasn't back there in the dark.

It wasn't.

The Apache helicopter had fallen behind some boxes and the fishing line was all knotted and tangled but luck-ily nothing was broken. I picked it up and used part of my shirt to dust it off, figuring I could untangle the fishing line in my room where the light was better. Then I clicked the light off and hurried down the stairs before the shadows could jump out and get me.

Untangling the fishing line didn't take long and when I was done I got a sock from my dresser, put it on my hand, and wiped the rest of the dust off the helicopter. Then I took the chopper into the bathroom, got a Q-tip, and cleaned the spaces in between the missiles where they attached to the wing pylons and where the rotors snapped into the body—anywhere I hadn't been able to reach with my dusting sock. I held the helicopter up and the light seemed to bounce off of it. I'd swear it was cleaner than it had been when my dad and I had first put it together.

I went back to my room, sat at my desk, and went through my drawers until I found my modeling paints and a brush. Using white paint, I very carefully wrote the word 'Buttercup' underneath the cockpit on both sides, twisting the bristles into a point with my fingers each time before dipping it in the paint so the letters would be sharper. It was taking a long time but I stuck with it. I mean, drawing the scales on the piranhadiles had been harder and this meant way more to me than that did. After the paint was dry I stood on my bed and put the helicopter back on its hook. I looked at it for a while as it twisted slowly back and forth and was so focused on it I almost didn't hear the tapping at the door.

"Derek?" Aunt Josie said. "You've been up here for a while. Everything okay?"

"Yup."

"Can I come in?"

I opened the door and we looked at each other for a moment or two without saying anything. Aunt Josie searched my face while I looked at the ring in her nostril, deciding it must've hurt when she got it even though she'd said it hadn't. She must have found what she was looking for because she smiled. ·

"You've got some updog on your shirt," she said.

"What's updog?"

"Not much, what's up with you?"

"Hardly har-har."

"Isn't it *hardy* har-har?"

"Not this time."

"Ouch," she said. "Hey, what's that paint all over your hands?"

"I was painting my Apache helicopter. Y'know—the one Dad and I built? The one Mom took down without asking? I painted 'Buttercup' on it."

"You painted flowers on a war helicopter?"

"I painted the *word* 'Buttercup.' That's her name. Dad said so in the letter."

I showed *Buttercup* to Aunt Josie and I showed her the photograph. I didn't show her the letter though, because it was private and none of her business. But not in a bad way. She told me I did a killer job on the lettering and that a lot of tattoo artists didn't like to do it because it was really tough to get just right.

"I've gotta get dinner started," she said. "Wanna come give me a hand? I totally get it if you don't want to though."

I told her I'd be down in a few minutes and she gave me a hug and said okay. When she was gone I hung *Buttercup* back on her hook, lay down on my bed, and watched her swing. When she stopped moving I went downstairs and found Aunt Josie in the kitchen chopping carrots, humming along to a song on the radio.

"What're you listening to?"

"Oingo Boingo," she said. "C'mon—dance with me!"

"What? No, wait . . . what are you doing?"

"The Shopping Cart."

"What?"

"You've never heard of the—oh, you poor boy."

She showed me how to do the Shopping Cart. And the Sprinkler. And my favorite—the Fisherman. Then we just held hands and twirled around the kitchen and even though I hadn't wanted to dance at first I was kinda sad when the song ended and we stopped. I grabbed a piece of carrot off the cutting board and popped it in my mouth.

"Save some for the salad, please," she said.

Aunt Josie picked up the cutting board and dumped the carrots into a big bowl that already had lettuce and sliced cucumber in it. She scratched the side of her nose and stared into the salad.

"What's missing? What's missing?" she mumbled. "Blue cheese!"

Aunt Josie opened the fridge and practically dove inside. I hoisted myself onto the counter, sat, and snagged a carrot from the salad bowl, popping it into my mouth and chewing quickly.

"Blue cheese, blue cheese . . . I could've sworn . . . aha!"

Aunt Josie emerged from the fridge with a plastic container. Then she pulled the lid off and shook some crumbled cheese into the salad bowl.

"Wait! Stop!" I said. "I think the cheese went bad."

"It didn't."

"But it looks all moldy."

"That's because it *is* moldy."

"Aunt Josie?"

"Yes?"

"Is there anything else for dinner?"

Before Josie could answer, a song by something called The Jam came on and we were dancing again.

The good news was that, in addition to the salad, Aunt Josie had also made baked ziti. The bad news was that she said I had to eat some salad anyway. I did a pretty good job of picking out the cheese but a couple times I ate some cucumber that tasted a little bit like feet so I obviously didn't get all of it.

After dinner me and Aunt Josie did the dishes then went into the living room and put on the TV. We played rocks, paper, scissors to see who got the remote control and I won because Aunt Josie always threw scissors first. I flipped through the kid channels but couldn't find anything I wanted to watch or hadn't already seen like a hundred times already so I handed over the remote.

"Can I stay up until Mom gets home?"

"I don't see why not," said Aunt Josie. "Do me a favor, though? Could you get all ready for bed first?"

I sprang up and tore through the kitchen and up the stairs. I changed into my pajamas and put a sweatshirt on and went to the bathroom and brushed my teeth and was back downstairs before the commercials were even over. I flopped down on the couch and pulled the blanket over me because it was a little chilly even with the fire going.

I snuggled in against Aunt Josie and put my head on her shoulder. Then she tucked the blanket in around us and we watched a show where all the men wore ties and everyone smoked cigarettes and acted very serious and there weren't any car chases or zombies or anything. It would have been way better with zombies. Everything's better with zombies. I closed my eyes and thought about how cool it would be if there was a show with zombies who got into car chases.

"Derek?" Mom's voice. Her hand. Warm. Shaking me gently. "Wake up, Piggy-pig."

"Time izzit?"

"It's late, sweetie. Come on up to your room. Here, lean on me."

Mom scooped me off the couch and put her arm around my shoulders and steered me up the stairs to my bedroom. Then she helped me into bed and tucked me in and sat, brushing the hair off my forehead.

"I've been thinking about you," she said. "Are you okay?"

"Mm-hm."

"What was in the letter?"

"Words."

Mom was quiet for a minute. It was warm in my bed. I was comfy and Mom's fingers in my hair felt good. I drifted. Mom said something. I almost didn't hear it.

"Whuzzat?"

"I just asked if the letter said what you needed it to."

I opened my eyes. The door was open and a rectangle of light fell into my room from the hallway casting all sorts of shadows. These shadows weren't scary, though. These shadows were familiar. I knew all about these shadows.

I thought about Dad's letter—about all of Dad's letters—and how, in one way or another, they've always said exactly what I needed them to. I knew which ones to read if I needed cheering up. I knew which ones would make me feel good about myself and which ones would make me feel like I could conquer the world. I knew which one to read when I forgot Mom's birthday. I remembered what Budgie said about how even when my dad wasn't here, he was still here—how our letters kept us connected.

"Are you cold?" Mom asked.

"No. Why?"

"You're shaking."

My eyes prickled with tears and deep inside me it felt like something was trying very hard to get out. I took a deep breath. Mom had taken her hand off my head but still sat on the edge of the bed looking down at me. I was grateful for the dark. If she could see my tears she didn't say anything. There wasn't really any need to. We were both sad and we both knew why. We'd probably both be sad for a while.

"It was a good letter," I said finally.

She moved a little and I could tell she was smiling even though her face was covered in shadows.

"I'm glad. We'll get through all of this, I promise."

"I know. There's a solution to everything. Even if it's not clear at first."

"Where'd you hear that?"

"Dad said it in the letter."

"Well, your dad's right. There is a solution to everything," she said. "I'm right down the hall if you need me, okay? I love you, Derek. Very, very much."

"I love you, too, Mom."

She gave me another kiss, stood, and walked out of the room, leaving the door cracked a little to let some light in.

I pulled the quilt up around my chin and stared up at *Buttercup*. In the half-dark I could just make out the Hellfire missiles underneath the wings. I imagined I could see her name painted in white under the cockpit and as my eyelids began to get heavy I heard a noise—soft at first but getting louder and louder until my head was filled with the sound of rotor blades chopping the air apart.

I'm buzzing over a mountain range wearing one of those old leather flight helmets with the goggles fixed over my eyes. The glare off the snowcapped peaks is blinding. Something is different. I'm sitting up front in the gunner's seat and I never sit up front in the gunner's seat because I'm not the gunner. I crane my neck back and forth, trying to see behind me but I'm buckled in tightly and can't turn around all the way.

"Is anyone back there? Hello?"

My voice cracks, like when I'm trying not to cry or I'm scared. I'm not though. At least I don't think I am. I tell myself that the reason my hands are shaking is because it's cold.

I hear a crackling in my headset—the kind you hear when somebody's about to say something and I listen hard for what seems like forever and then I hear the crackling noise again, which means the person on the other end is done talking even though I didn't get to hear what they were saying.

"I can't—I didn't hear you! Hello?"

My headset crackles again and I close my eyes, suddenly remembering this thing Budgie said one time about blind people having superhuman hearing abilities and even though I don't believe him I figure it can't hurt to try.

The voice in my headset is a familiar one—one I haven't heard in a long time. I keep my eyes closed, as if opening them would allow it to escape.

"Hey, Kiddo," says Dad. "Mind if I fly for a while?"

So we fly like that—me up front in the gunner's seat and Dad in the pilot's seat behind me. The sky is big and endless and empty. No Japanese Zeros fall toward us out of the sun. We aren't a pair of sitting ducks, caught in the Luftwaffe's crosshairs. Not today.

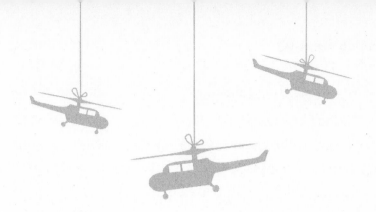

THE NEXT DAY AFTER lunch Aunt Josie had to go to the mall and I had to go with her. Mom was working and I wasn't allowed to stay alone in the house for that long, which I didn't really understand. I mean, it wasn't like the chances of something happening increased by the half-hour or anything. I was just as likely to play with matches ten minutes after being left alone as I was after an hour. I didn't feel like arguing though so I shuffled a few steps behind Aunt Josie with my hands stuffed into my pockets and my eyes on her feet in front of me, thinking about all the TV I was missing.

"Derek!"

"What?"

"Did you hear what I said?"

"It's time to go home?"

"No. I said I need to exchange a few things in this store. You can come in but I'm warning you right now—it's pretty girly. Do you want to wait out here for me?"

"Can I go get a doughnut?"

"I don't know."

"Come on, the food court's *right there*. I'll get a doughnut and come right back, okay? I won't be two seconds."

She caved then and agreed to my terms with the condition that I bring her back a doughnut as well but I was so excited about the prospect of freedom that I forgot which kind she wanted. I figured I'd just get her something with pink frosting. Or sprinkles. I was pretty sure Aunt Josie liked sprinkles.

I took my time walking down to the food court because I liked the way my reflection looked in the store windows without Mom or Aunt Josie right there with me. I looked independent—a free man at the mall just minding his own business. And if this man's business happened to involve doughnuts, then nobody could say boo. Even if one of them *did* end up being pink and sprinkly.

I got in line at Mojo Donuts and started to check out the selection, but after two minutes the only concrete decision I'd made was to return as soon as humanly possible with more money and buy the place out. I ended up getting a lemon glazed French cruller for Aunt Josie and something called Da Bomb for me. It was a cream-filled chocolate doughnut with chocolate frosting and mini chocolate chips with a red licorice fuse.

The doughnuts were boxed up separately and put into a white paper bag. I took it and as I was leaving recognized someone sitting at one of the tables. There was an open Mojo Donut box in front of her with a partly eaten doughnut inside. Raspberry filled? How had I missed that one? Her nose was in a book. As usual.

"Hey, Violet!"

"Derek! Hi! What are you doing here?"

"Getting doughnuts."

"Are you here with someone?" she asked.

"My aunt's exchanging some stuff and I got hungry so, y'know . . . you?"

"My dad's in the photo booth," she said. "You can sit down if you want."

"What's he need pictures for?" I said, sliding into the chair across from her.

"He needs a new passport."

"Where's he going?"

"Wales."

"Cool. Is he going to see all of them?"

"All of what?"

"All of the whales. There's a lot of them."

"Not the *mammals*," she said, smiling. Her nose crinkled a little, making her freckles crash into each other. She only had one dimple. It was awesome. "The country."

"Oh."

Me and Violet sat there for a minute and didn't say anything. She picked at her doughnut a little, breaking a piece off and scooting it around in the raspberry filling before eating it.

"He's going to be gone for three months."

"Three months? That's easy. When my dad was gone I'd sometimes hold my breath for three months."

"I know it's not that long," she said. "Plus I get to go visit over February vacation."

"See? At least you're *allowed* to visit. I woulda loved to visit my dad but no—it's too dangerous, they said. There's a war going on, they said."

Violet laughed a little, then got quiet.

"I was sorry to hear about your father, Derek," she said softly. "I meant to tell you earlier but never got a chance."

It was my turn to get quiet. I stared at her doughnut and only then realized how much the raspberry filling looked like blood. I shrugged. Nodded. Mumbled "Thanks."

"I didn't mean to make you sad."

"That's okay."

"The funny thing is that just when you think you're going to be sad the rest of your life you wake up one morning and you're not sad anymore."

"How would you know? Your dad hasn't even left yet."

I didn't mean to say those words. Well, maybe I did—I just hadn't meant for them to come out sounding so mean. Violet didn't flinch or anything. She just sat there looking at me, making me wonder if I'd spoken out loud at all.

"My mom passed away, Derek," she said. "That's how I know."

"No she didn't."

"Yes she did. Three years ago."

"But she was at the play."

"That was my stepmom."

"Crap."

Violet smiled. She actually *smiled*. It made me feel a little better. Not great—just less bad.

"What happened to your mom?"

"She got sick."

"My dad's helicopter was shot down."

"I know," she said. "It was on the news."

"You saw that?"

"A lot of people did," she said. "My dad read it in the paper."

"It still doesn't seem real."

"It will. And it'll hurt. But you'll get through it. I did."

"How?"

"It wasn't any one thing. I mean, life just kept going. We still got mail every day. I still had homework to do. People kept playing tennis and driving their cars and walking their dogs. I couldn't get mad at them for living their lives just because I was sad. And in a strange way that's when I started feeling better."

"Welcome to Dragsville, Ohio."

"What?"

"It's something my dad used to say."

"Your father sounds funny."

"He was."

"Violet, sweetheart, who's your friend?"

I jumped a little. I'd been so busy thinking about my father that I wasn't aware of Violet's until he was standing right next to me. I stood and we shook hands.

"Derek Lamb, sir. Violet and I are in the same class."

"It's good to meet you, Derek," he said. "Lamb, Lamb . . . where have I—oh, from the play!"

"Yes sir."

"That was a heck of a thing, wasn't it? The punch-up there in the beginning? I've always said that nothing spices up a classic like a good donnybrook."

"Huh?"

"He's just playing with you, Derek," said Violet. "Dad, cut it out."

"She's right. I'm joking," he said. "Violet, are you ready to go?"

Violet carefully closed the lid to the Mojo Donut box. Then she put her book away in her backpack, stood up, and to my surprise gave me a hug. Her hair tickled my nose as I hugged her back. It felt different than it had in the play—like there was something more to it. I found myself not wanting it to end and I didn't care if there was anyone from school around to see it. Even Budgie.

"See you in school, Derek," she said.

Then she got her bag, took her father's hand, and left the food court, not skipping but looking as though she might at any moment. She turned around once to wave good-bye. I waved back and stood there for a moment. Thinking. Then I remembered the deal I'd made with Aunt Josie so I grabbed my doughnut bag and started back to meet her.

I didn't look at my reflection in the windows this time because I was too busy thinking about Violet and the way she'd hugged me. And the more I thought about it the surer I was that it hadn't been just a hug. It had been an embrace. Definitely. Violet had *embraced* me.

My head was swimming with the smell of her hair.

Apples. Her hair smelled like apples.

Tomorrow must be Saturday.

Acknowledgments

I WOULD LIKE to thank the good folks at Grub Street in Boston for helping me get started and the lovely and talented Joanna Cardenas at Penguin for helping me to finish. I also owe an enormous debt of gratitude (and cookies) to my agent, George Nicholson, for everything in between. Much love to Luke Farrell, Sgt. Jason Macauly, and LTC Eric Frizzell. Finally, I want to thank my wife, Kara, who believes.